*Harlequin is thrilled to welcome
Vicki Lewis Thompson back to Blaze.*

**Look what people are saying about this
talented author's latest works.**

"Vicki Lewis Thompson gives readers
a sexy, funny tale."
—*Romance Reviews Today* on
Better Naughty than Nice

"Hang on for the ride of your life...
I could not put this book down!"
—*Night Owl Reviews* on *Blonde with a Wand*

"If you thought *Over Hexed* was phenomenal,
wait until you read *Wild & Hexy!*...
a rip-roaring good time."
—*Romance Junkies*

"The same trademark blend of comedy
and heart that won Thompson's Nerd
series a loyal following."
—*Publishers Weekly* on *Over Hexed*

"Thompson mixes magic, small-town quirkiness,
and passionate sex for a winsome effect."
—*Booklist* on *Over Hexed*

Blaze™

Dear Reader,

Welcome back to the Last Chance Ranch! The town of Shoshone, a small community that's part of the Jackson Hole region in Wyoming, is celebrating the Fourth of July, and the Last Chance always has an entry in the parade. So let's grab a lawn chair and stake out a spot along Main Street.

There's nothing like a parade on the Fourth to stir up a little patriotism! And what represents the spirit of this fine country better than cowboys in snug jeans riding magnificent horses? Save me a seat, because I don't want to miss a thing, especially when the Last Chance entry arrives.

All three Chance men plan to ride those spectacular registered paints they breed at the ranch. Jack, the oldest, will be mounted on his black-and-white stallion Bandit, while Nick, the middle son, has chosen his dad's favorite, a butterscotch paint named Gold Rush. Gabe, the youngest, will no doubt be riding Top Drawer, a handsome roan paint.

Nick's fiancée Dominique is in town for the long weekend, but Jack and Gabe are still unattached. As they ride by, you may hear sighs of longing from the single women along the parade route. It's understandable that they'd entertain a few fantasies about the Chance men. After all, guys like these are what made this country great. Come on, the parade's about to start!

Patriotically yours,

Vicki

Vicki Lewis
Thompson

AMBUSHED!

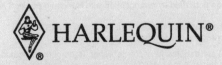

HARLEQUIN®

TORONTO • NEW YORK • LONDON
AMSTERDAM • PARIS • SYDNEY • HAMBURG
STOCKHOLM • ATHENS • TOKYO • MILAN • MADRID
PRAGUE • WARSAW • BUDAPEST • AUCKLAND

Recycling programs
for this product may
not exist in your area.

ISBN-13: 978-0-373-79554-3

AMBUSHED!

To the undaunted residents of Summerhaven, a small mountain town in Arizona that survived a devastating forest fire in 2004 and has proudly risen from the ashes. Your annual Fourth of July parade is a testament to your resilience and creativity.

Prologue

June 3, 1937
From the diary of Eleanor Chance

WHO WOULD have thought sex in a hayloft could be so much fun? Or that I'd be happy living in a barn? But the barn was in better shape than the house when we arrived at the Last Chance Ranch a month ago, so Archie and I took the hayloft for our bedroom and my brother Seth sleeps in one of the stalls down below.

I won't pretend the past month's been easy for me, what with learning to be a bride and a carpenter all at once. Archie says I'm pretty good at being a bride. The two of us burn up the sheets in our makeshift bed. But even Archie, who loves me dearly, admits I'm a little less talented as a carpenter.

Fortunately Seth is better at that skill than I am. Between Archie and Seth's efforts and my puny contributions, we've made a temporary home out of the barn and have a start on building a house. We tore down the old one, with much hooting and hollering because it was such an eyesore.

If we work like beavers we might have the house done before the first snow, which would be nice. Winters are hard in Jackson Hole, and besides, I'd like to celebrate Christmas in a real house instead of a barn.

Even though I'm not so great with a hammer, my sewing has helped us out. I made a wedding dress for a nearby rancher's daughter and took a cow in payment. The barter system works well here, and eventually I hope to stitch my way to another four-legged critter. This time I want a bull. Archie and I are holding off starting a family until we have an income-producing cattle herd.

More news—Seth has taken a liking to Joyce, the woman who owns the Rusty Spur Saloon in nearby Shoshone. Seth can't afford but one beer a night, so he makes it last and flirts like crazy with Joyce.

She's a good woman and I know Seth is looking for the same kind of happiness Archie and I have. Archie's given me a nickname. He calls me Nelsie. I like it.

In between the carpentering, Archie helped me plant a vegetable garden. We're out in the middle of nowhere, so he had to fence it to keep out the rabbits and deer. The tomato vines have blossomed and carrot tops are waving in the breeze.

It's funny, but that garden seems almost as important as having a roof over my head. I feel like I'm putting down roots right along with the vegetables. Against all odds, we're building a life here. I do believe this is where we are meant to be.

1

Present Day

GABE CHANCE hadn't expected to get all choked up over riding in Shoshone's annual Fourth of July parade. For the past ten years he'd spent summers competing in cutting-horse events and hadn't been home to take part in this nonsense. But he was home now and it was the first parade without his dad. Milling around the staging area without Jonathan Chance barking orders seemed plain wrong.

His two older brothers were pretending they weren't affected. That was easier for Jack, who was four years ahead of Gabe and eons ahead of the human race in his ability to hide his feelings. Nick was struggling a bit. Gabe could see it in his green eyes. As for their mom—well, Sarah had chosen to wear shades for the occasion. Good call.

Thank God Jack had vetoed Nick's typically sappy idea of tying Gold Rush, their dad's butterscotch paint, behind the Last Chance wagon driven by Emmett Sterling, the ranch foreman. Talk about maudlin. As a compromise, Nick was riding Gold Rush, because a Fourth of July parade wouldn't seem right without that flashy horse prancing down Main Street.

Nick kept close to the wagon because his main squeeze, Dominique Jeffries, was riding in it. She was a photographer based in Indiana and was only here for the long weekend, but from the way those two lovebirds were acting, Gabe predicted she'd soon relocate.

Naturally she was shooting a bunch of pictures of Nick on that horse. She'd never met their dad, so she had no reason to be sentimental today, but every time Gabe looked over at Gold Rush all tricked out in his dad's silver-studded saddle, a baseball-size lump clogged his throat. He needed a distraction and he needed one now.

Well, hallelujah. Just beyond the staging area a gorgeous redhead was struggling to control an Appaloosa. The gelding first tried brushing her off against a post. Then he headed for a patch of grass several yards away and paid no attention as she attempted to steer him back.

Gabe rose in his stirrups and pointed to the redhead as he hollered over at Jack. "I'm gonna help her out. I'll be right back."

Jack gave him a stern look that was pure Jonathan Chance, Senior. "Don't get lost. Parade starts in fifteen minutes."

"I'll be here." Gabe wasn't crazy about the way Jack was issuing orders these days, but their dad's will had put his oldest brother solidly in charge of the ranch. That set Jack and Gabe on a collision course, because suddenly Jack was questioning whether the Last Chance should fund Gabe's cutting-horse events.

Their dad had always said that Gabe's presence on the circuit boosted sales of the ranch's registered paints, and Gabe's horse Top Drawer was only ten grand shy of the required earnings for the American Cutting Horse Association's Hall of Fame. But apparently Jack viewed Gabe's summers away as a drain on the system. Maybe the lack of support was affecting Gabe's concentration, because he wasn't winning as much prize money on Top Drawer this summer, which made for a vicious cycle.

He'd unwittingly brought the issue to a head during an unscheduled trip home with an injured mare he'd saved from the slaughterhouse. Jack had seized the opportunity to keep Gabe at the ranch for a while.

Gabe figured he could change his brother's attitude eventually, but for today he'd set the conflict aside. It was a holiday, one that made them all super-aware that their dad was gone. He'd try to keep the peace, mostly for his mother's sake.

But that didn't mean he couldn't walk Top Drawer over and assist the redhead battling a gelding that didn't seem to like parades. Because Gabe was following the woman, he had a chance to read the embroidered back of her white satin Western shirt. Morgan O'Connelli Real Estate.

He recognized that strange last name from somewhere. He even remembered that it was a weird-ass combination of Irish and Italian created by parents who hadn't wanted to hyphenate their kids' last names. But he wasn't sure why he knew that.

Before he had a chance to reach the woman, the

Appaloosa took a notion and started to trot, nearly dislodging her. She lost her cool but not her seat, although clearly she was now merely a passenger and the horse was in charge, probably headed back to the barn.

Gabe nudged Top Drawer into a canter. Luckily he'd chosen to ride this particular horse today. The roan paint had some thoroughbred in him and was much faster than Finicky, Gabe's other cutting horse.

When the Appaloosa gathered his speckled hindquarters and put on his own burst of speed, Gabe decided he was done playing games. Leaning over Top Drawer's neck, he urged his horse on and caught up to the gelding easily. "Hang on!" he called to the woman as he came up on her left.

She abandoned the reins and gripped the saddle horn.

Grabbing the Appaloosa's bridle, Gabe braced himself. "Whoa, son! Whoa, there!"

The horse slowed in tandem with Top Drawer, proving that he was schooled well enough, but had chosen to take advantage of an inexperienced rider. The two horses stopped in the middle of the empty street.

"That's better." Switching his grip from the Appaloosa's bridle to the knotted reins hanging around the horse's neck, Gabe glanced over at the redhead to see how she was holding up. "You okay?"

She flashed him a big smile, but her jaw was clenched tighter than a strap on a hay bale and her face was almost as white as her shirt. "Fine!" She barely moved her lips.

He decided she was in shock. "Stay right there and I'll come get you."

"Fine!" She had a deer-in-the-headlights look and only a faint ring of blue-green showed around her dilated pupils.

Keeping a firm grip on the Appaloosa's reins, Gabe maneuvered Top Drawer until he had room to dismount. Then he ground-tied his horse so he could concentrate on helping the redhead out of the saddle.

She had a death-grip on the saddle horn and was breathing fast, fast enough that she drew Gabe's attention to the front of her shirt. He had a special fondness for big-breasted women, but he knew it was politically incorrect, not to mention rude, to let his gaze linger there. Still, he couldn't help noticing that the top three snaps were undone and a fourth was threatening to pop any minute.

He glanced up at her. "Ready to come down?"

"Sure!" She favored him with another big smile.

"Want any help?"

"No, thanks!" Without any preliminaries she swung her right leg over the horse's spotted rump. But the Appaloosa was tall and she wasn't, so unless she loosened her grip on that horn...

As the dismount started going bad, Gabe stepped in and caught her around the waist. "Easy does it."

Just then he heard a pop and figured the fourth snap had given up the ghost.

"Shitfire!"

He bit the inside of his cheek to keep from laughing as he set her on her booted feet with her back to him. Then he stepped away so she had the privacy to refasten her shirt.

In between muttered swear words, she clicked the

snap. "Stupid shirt's one size smaller than I ordered. By the time it came in the mail, I didn't have time to get another one."

"These things happen," he murmured.

"There!" She spun to face him and she most definitely had her game face on. "Now I can properly thank you for riding to my rescue, Gabriel Chance. That was awesome."

"You know my name?" He gazed into eyes that were neither green nor blue. He was reminded of the turquoise of tribal jewelry, and again, a memory stirred. He'd swear they'd met before.

"Everybody knows the Chance boys. But besides that, we had one semester together at JHHS our junior year."

"You're Morgan O'Connelli!" He pronounced her surname with an emphasis on the last two syllables, as an Italian would.

"That's me. The daughter of Seamus O'Conner and Bianca Spinelli, the infamous pair who created the confusing last name of O'Connelli, thereby assuring that their children would suffer through each and every class roll call."

"But it's distinctive." She hadn't changed it, either, so she must not hate it that much. Now that he knew who she was, Gabe started sifting back through his memories. "Didn't we work on the junior-senior prom together?"

"We did. We spent the afternoon before the prom blowing up helium balloons and sniffing a little gas now and then so we could sing like the Chipmunks."

"Yeah." He laughed. Just like that, everything about

her came back to him—vagabond parents, modern-day gypsies, really, who drifted from one place to another in an old van. A passel of kids, maybe seven or eight. Morgan had been the oldest. Enrolling in the middle of junior year, when most of the class had lived in the Jackson Hole area all their lives, must have been tough.

But she'd thrown herself into school activities with a vengeance, volunteering for all the little jobs nobody else wanted. He'd been going steady with someone at the time, so he couldn't ask her out. Besides, the word around school was that she couldn't date much because she babysat her younger brothers and sisters.

Gabe hadn't allowed himself to think about her in romantic terms, yet he remembered those eyes and that flame-red hair. If he wanted to be perfectly honest with himself, he'd have to admit he also remembered her rack. She'd almost been accepted as part of the gang, and then…she was gone.

"I remember you worked at the diner for a while after school was out that summer."

"Uh-huh. I *loved* making shakes. And it was a great excuse to get out of babysitting."

He'd loved watching her in that little white uniform, but he didn't say that. "I went in there one day and they said you'd left."

"That was right before the Fourth of July celebration," she said. "And speaking of that, you'd better get back or you'll be late." She unclipped a cell phone from her tooled leather belt. "I'll call the stable and tell them to come get this nag. I'm afraid Geronimo is a parade washout, at least with me on board. Oh, well." She shrugged. *"Chi non risica, non rosica."*

He knew absolutely no Italian. "Which means?"

"Nothing ventured, nothing gained."

Gabe wasn't fooled. Her cheerful acceptance of her fate didn't ring true. From what he remembered of her, she loved to be part of things and a Fourth-of-July parade would be right up her alley.

"Don't call them," he said. "We'll just switch horses."

She paused in the act of dialing. "That's very generous, but I couldn't possibly accept."

"Don't you want to ride in the parade?"

"Well, sure, but I don't think I quite realized how tricky it would be."

"So this is your first parade?"

She smiled. "Yep. I'm a parade virgin."

"Then we need to change your status today." And if their discussion had sexual overtones, he didn't mind a bit. She'd started it.

Still smiling, she shook her head. "I'll bet your horse is worth a gazillion dollars."

"Doesn't matter." Gabe thought Jack might say it mattered a lot, but Top Drawer was Gabe's horse and he could loan out the roan paint if he wanted to. That meant Gabe would be riding an Appaloosa instead of one of the Last Chance paints, and Jack might not like that, either. The ranch used the parade to showcase their registered horses, so in the past their entry had been all paints, all the time. But Gabe wasn't in the mood to please Jack right now.

"No, really, Gabe. If anything were to happen to him,

or to someone in the parade while I'm riding him, I'd never forgive myself."

"Nothing will happen." Gabe gestured toward his horse. Top Drawer hadn't moved since Gabe had dropped the reins to the ground. "He's trained within an inch of his life. You won't have a single problem, but if you're worried, you can ride next to me."

Eagerness gleamed in her eyes for a moment before she looked away. "I *really* appreciate the offer. You don't know how much." She glanced back at him. "But it wouldn't be right."

"Why not?"

"I'd be horning in on your parade entry, interrupting your family event, insinuating myself into a situation that isn't my—"

"Aw, hell, Morgan. You know you want to do it, so just get on my horse and make it snappy or we'll both be late."

She hesitated another second and then grinned. "Okay, Gabe. You're right. I really do want to be in this parade. I've been thinking about it ever since... well, since I was sixteen, I guess."

Thank God he'd offered. "Then let's do it."

"I'll be forever in your debt."

"Yeah? That sounds promising."

She laughed. "Don't get all excited. Opening a business has sucked up most of my capital. But I might be able to swing dinner at Spirits and Spurs if you avoid the steak." She walked over to Top Drawer and scrambled aboard. The fourth snap on her shirt popped open again.

Instantly Gabe thought of another way she could

show her gratitude, and immediately felt like a jerk. He was doing a good deed and expected nothing in return. Absolutely nothing.

"Damnation." She pulled the shirt together and snapped it.

Doing his level best not to stare, Gabe led the Appaloosa over so he could hold on to the wayward horse while he adjusted her stirrups. No doubt being turned on by a glimpse of her spectacular cleavage reflected poorly on his character.

But there you had it. He was superficial and immature enough to wish that snap would stay open.

"Oh, would you please get my little purse?" she asked. "I left it tied around the saddle horn, and I doubt you'll want to ride in the parade with it hanging there in full view."

"That would be a negative." He fetched the small leather purse, no bigger than a wallet, and handed it up to her.

As she reached for it, the snap popped again. "This is getting annoying."

"Maybe you should give up and leave it undone." He figured every guy along the parade route would be grateful.

She looped the purse strap over the saddle horn and snapped her shirt together again. "Now you sound like my mother—*if you've got it, flaunt it.*"

"Your mom said that?" Gabe couldn't imagine that sentence ever crossing *his* mother's lips, especially in relation to one of her kids.

"She's Italian," Morgan said, as if that explained everything.

Gabe thought about that as he lengthened his stirrups and mounted up. Kids tended to take after their parents, and obviously Morgan had inherited her red hair and blue-green eyes from her Irish dad, a guy he'd met once at some school function her parents had attended. What had she inherited from her hot-blooded, dark-haired Italian mother? A passionate nature?

In high school he'd been unavailable, but it happened that he was fancy-free at the moment. Even though he expected nothing in return for this good deed, he wasn't about to refuse if Morgan wanted to renew their friendship. This horse trade might turn out to be one of his better moves.

2

EVEN A dedicated optimist like Morgan couldn't have predicted that renting that stubborn horse Geronimo would have an upside—a rather spectacular upside, in fact. Although she was a little nervous about busting in on the Chance family's event, she'd been invited by one of the crown princes to do exactly that. She thought of the Chances as Shoshone's royal family.

Gabe certainly carried himself like royalty, his posture relaxed and easy in the saddle as he rode beside her to the parade staging area. Morgan had never known one of the Chance boys to look nervous, and why should they? They all had a strong sense of self, a trait she was working hard to make part of her personality.

She'd admired Gabe from the day she'd arrived at JHHS twelve years ago. No, *admired* was too tame a word. She'd had a crush the size of the Teton Mountain Range. Of course, she'd had no shot back then. As president of the junior class and star running back, Gabe Chance could have had almost any girl in school. He'd been going steady with somebody named Jennifer.

Amazingly, he now appeared to be unattached. With

his all-American good looks, sandy hair and laughing blue eyes, she would have expected him to be off the market. Instead he'd asked her to ride with him in the parade, and that didn't seem like the act of a man with a girlfriend.

He'd also been very interested in her tight shirt. She gave him points for not openly staring, though. She'd suffered through her share of ogling and crude remarks over the years. As a young teen she'd wished for smaller breasts, but eventually she'd learned to accept, even be grateful for the body she had.

Her generous measurements provided a terrific litmus test to see whether a guy had any class. Although she couldn't expect men to ignore her double-Ds, she appreciated any effort at subtlety. Gabe had made that effort.

Come to think of it, he'd done the same back in high school, too. The afternoon of the prom he'd helped her inflate more than a hundred balloons and had never once made a comparison between the balloons and her girls. She'd fallen a little bit more in love with him that day.

She didn't mind showing off her assets under certain circumstances, but riding in a family-oriented parade wasn't one of them. When the embroidered shirt she'd ordered had arrived a size too small, she'd considered not wearing it, but then she'd have no way to advertise her business. Advertising was her excuse for riding, although it wasn't the reason.

She'd dreamed about this parade and the festivities that followed from the moment she'd been denied the experience as a teenager. During the brief time she'd lived in this town, she'd felt a connection, as if this was where she was ultimately supposed to wind up. She'd hated to leave and had vowed to come back.

It had taken her some time to honor that vow, what with working her way through college and figuring out what she wanted to be when she grew up. Once she'd qualified for her real estate license, she'd worked in Jackson until she'd felt confident enough to open her own office in Shoshone two months ago.

Spending the Fourth of July here marked the beginning of her new life, a life where she would put down roots at last. And she'd be helping others to put down roots by selling houses. She was all about the concept of *home*.

Meeting Gabe Chance today was a bonus she hadn't counted on, though. But then, once a girl set out to build the life she wanted, anything could happen. She could find herself riding down the street with the man of her dreams.

At least he had been the man of her dreams twelve years ago. She probably needed to find out a little bit more about him before she cast him in that role now. And at some point, she wanted to express her condolences. She knew he'd lost his dad the previous year.

She settled for a neutral conversational gambit. "So what have you been up to since high school?"

He glanced over at her. "Got a degree in business, but mostly I've concentrated on my riding. Top Drawer is one of two cutting horses I use in competition."

She had no trouble picturing him out there in the ring, doing himself proud. "I'll bet you're good at it."

"Top Drawer is good at it. I just try not to interfere."

So he hadn't developed a big head in the years since she'd first met him. He'd been a fierce competitor back then, but not a braggart. She was happy that hadn't changed.

"And I'm sure you're also promoting the Last Chance paints when you ride," she said.

"I think so, and my dad used to think so, but Jack may take some convincing."

"I'm not sure I've ever met Jack."

"You may not have. He'd finished high school by then, and that was about the time my dad was getting out of the cattle business and switching over to selling paint horses. He needed Jack to help during the transition."

She had her opening and she took it. "I was so sorry to hear about your dad."

"Yeah, it was unexpected."

"I'm sure." Last fall she'd been working for a broker in Jackson when she'd heard Jonathan Chance had been killed in a rollover. By that time the funeral was over and she probably wouldn't have gone, anyway. She hadn't ever met Jonathan and wasn't sure if Gabe or Nick would remember her.

Within a month of the accident, Morgan's broker had gone down to Shoshone to leave his card in case Jonathan's widow decided to sell the ranch. Morgan had been happy to hear that wasn't going to happen, both for the family's sake and for hers. When she moved to Shoshone, she wanted the community to be just as she remembered it, which included having the Chances still in residence.

Thinking about that now, she realized the parade would be the first one since Jonathan's death. "Gabe, I'm a little slow on the uptake, but this isn't the time for you to bring a stranger into a family event. You probably have enough to deal with."

His glance was warm. "That's considerate of you, Morgan, but in the first place, you're not a stranger. You're a friend from high school. In the second place, I think you're exactly what we need to keep from getting bogged down in nostalgia."

"Well, okay, but if anybody's unhappy about it, we can still switch horses and the parade can go on without me."

"That won't be happening." Gabe headed for the cluster of horses and riders near the Last Chance wagon. "Right this way, Miss O'Connelli. Let me introduce you."

Morgan took a deep breath, but not too deep. That damned snap was going to stay fastened or else. She should have used a safety pin, but the shirt was satin and would show pin holes.

Riding along with Gabe was one thing. She knew him, at least a little bit. But facing the entire family was a daunting experience. Still, she was good at daunting experiences. Being tossed from pillar to post as a kid meant she'd had to learn how to adjust to whatever circumstances she found herself in.

Her first line of defense was her smile, so she trotted out a happy grin once they were close enough for Gabe's family to notice.

Gabe started the introductions with a trim woman wearing a red Stetson, a Western shirt with red fringe, black jeans and red boots. Sleek white hair peeked out from under her hat but her eyes were covered by sunglasses.

"Mom," Gabe said, "I'd like you to meet an old friend from high school. This is Morgan O'Connelli. Morgan, this is my mother, Sarah."

Morgan kept her smile in place as she murmured a greeting.

Sarah returned the smile, but she seemed to be making an effort. "Nice to meet you, Morgan. You must be the new real estate agent in town."

"That's right." Judging from the way Sarah said the words *real estate agent,* Morgan had the distinct impression that wasn't a good thing. Maybe her broker hadn't been the only one knocking on Sarah's door after her husband's death. "Have you had problems with agents bothering you?"

"You have no idea."

Morgan cringed inwardly. "I'm sorry to hear that."

"It hasn't been fun."

"Just so you know, I have no interest in your property."

Sarah nodded without comment, and Morgan felt dismissed. Her usual charm wasn't working at all with this woman, but she could understand why. This had to be a tough day for Sarah, and she couldn't be happy having a rider in the group who was advertising a real estate agency on the back of her shirt.

"Hey, Morgan!" Nick, mounted on a butterscotch paint decked out in a silver-studded saddle, called over from his spot beside the wagon. "I wondered if that was you when the office opened."

"It's me!" Morgan was grateful for Nick's friendliness.

He tilted his head toward a woman sitting in the wagon. "This is my good friend Dominique Jeffries from Indiana."

Dominique's short, dark hair peeked out from under a wide-brimmed straw hat and she had an expensive-looking camera on a strap around her neck. She waved at Morgan, her expression cheerful. "Hi! Looks like you two traded horses."

Morgan started to explain but Gabe got there ahead of her.

"We had to," he said. "Otherwise Morgan wouldn't have been in the parade." Then he introduced the other woman in the wagon—Mary Lou Simms, the ranch cook—and the driver—Emmett Sterling, the ranch foreman. Mary Lou was in charge of throwing candy to the kids along the route.

Both Mary Lou and Emmett gave her a pleasant but reserved greeting. Morgan told herself that was natural, under the circumstances. But so far, only Nick and the woman who was probably his girlfriend had been truly friendly.

Finally Gabe looked over at a dark-haired cowboy on the far side of the wagon. He wore all black, and was mounted on a striking black-and-white paint.

Morgan had no doubt this was Jack, who was now the head of the Chance clan.

Gabe confirmed what she already knew as he introduced them. "Jack, meet Morgan. I've invited her to ride in the parade with us today."

Jack's eyes narrowed, but then he touched the brim of his hat. "Glad to have you, ma'am."

Morgan heard the words of welcome but didn't believe them for a second. Once Gabe had announced that she'd be riding with them, a decided chill had settled over the group. She kept her smile firmly in place. Maybe there was still time for her to return Gabe's horse and call the stables to fetch Geronimo.

"Time to move out!" Jack raised his hand like an old-fashioned trail boss.

So much for that. She'd have to see this through, hold her head high and keep her shirt snaps together.

"Morgan and I will follow Nick," Gabe said as the group started lining up behind Jack. That wasn't the order they'd planned on, but Gabe thought it was for the best.

When they'd talked about this the night before, his family had settled on having Jack lead, followed by their mother. Gabe was supposed to ride behind her, with the wagon next, and Nick at the end on Gold Rush as a sentimental tribute to their dad, who'd always been the entry's grand finale. But Gabe didn't want to be sandwiched in between his mother and the wagon in case Geronimo acted up or Morgan had any problems. He'd rather be at the end where there was a little room to maneuver before the next group came along.

Jack hesitated. "I don't..." Then he paused and shrugged. "Whatever. We need to go. Ready, Sarah?"

"Yes." She guided her roan paint, very similar to

Gabe's in color if not in markings, onto the parade route.

Next Emmett slapped the reins against the rumps of the two matched bay paints pulling the wagon, and it started off with a creak and a groan.

Nick glanced over at Gabe. "You're sure you want to be last in line?"

"Yep."

"All righty, then." Nick gave Gold Rush a nudge with his heels and the butterscotch paint, silver saddle winking in the sunlight, started after the wagon.

"Just stay on my right," Gabe said to Morgan. "We're going to be fine."

"You changed the order, didn't you?"

"A little."

Morgan kept her voice down. "This was a mistake."

"No, it wasn't." Gabe knew what she was talking about. Except for Nick and Dominique, the group had appeared less than thrilled about Morgan's presence. "It's just the real estate thing. It'll be fine. Wave."

"What?"

"Wave to the people on the sidewalk. It's what you do in a parade."

"Oh!" She immediately turned on the charm, swiveling in the saddle so that she could pay attention to the good citizens of Shoshone lining both sides of the street.

Meanwhile Gabe concentrated on keeping the pace slow. Mary Lou was throwing out wrapped candy, and kids scuffled for it. He watched carefully to make sure nobody ran toward the street.

"Hey, Gabe!" It was Elmer, who owned the town's only gas station. "What'cha doing riding an Appaloosa?"

"Just trying to be different!" Gabe called back.

"I didn't even think about *that*." Morgan kept smiling and waving, but she sounded upset. "Because of me, you're on the wrong kind of horse."

"Lighten up, Morgan. I'm not going to ruin the family's reputation with one ride on a different breed. Besides, you're supposed to be having fun losing your parade virginity, not obsessing about my rep."

That made her laugh. "I am having fun. Sort of."

"You'd better start having even more fun pretty soon. It's not a very long parade." He wished like hell his mom and Jack had been more enthusiastic about having Morgan, but he could understand why they weren't.

Morgan blew a few kisses to the crowd as she continued her conversation with Gabe. "So how bad was the real-estate-agent traffic around your house last fall?"

He blew out a breath. "Bad. After Dad died, a gazillion of them beat a path to our door with all kinds of dreams and schemes, thinking we'd want to sell all or part of the ranch and they'd make a bundle. They drove my mom crazy and the whole subject of real estate agents was taboo for months. Finally they quit calling."

"So your family thinks I'll do the same thing, now that I've met you and been invited to ride in the parade with them?"

"Maybe." And Gabe wasn't sure if she would or not. He hadn't thought that far. "Would you?"

"Absolutely not! I love the idea that your family has

owned that land for years. My parents never owned so much as a parking space for the van."

And he could tell that still bothered her, even now when she was an adult and didn't have to deal with their drifter ways. "Keep waving."

"Oh. Sorry." She went back to her parade duties.

"How are you liking the parade now?"

"Better. I wish I'd brought candy to throw out to the kids. I didn't think of it."

Gabe took advantage of a temporary halt and called out to Nick. "Hey, bro, can you snag a bag of candy from the wagon and pass it back?"

"Sure thing." Nick trotted forward, reached for the bag Mary Lou handed him and fell back until he was on Gabe's left. "Here you go." He handed the bag over to Gabe. "Gonna impress the rug rats?"

"Morgan wants to." Gabe held out the bag to her.

She took it with a smile. "Thanks! And thanks to you, too, Nick."

"My pleasure, Morgan." Nick touched the brim of his hat.

Gabe expected Nick to move back into his position ahead of them, but instead he stayed even with Gabe.

"Everything all right back here?" he asked.

"We're doing okay." Gabe glanced over at Morgan, who seemed totally absorbed in tossing candy to the kids. "Thanks for asking."

Nick lowered his voice. "You know it's the real estate thing."

"I know. I explained it to her."

"Did you also explain that she'd better not make a sales pitch for her services?"

"I didn't have to. She has great respect for the Chance family heritage, probably even more than I do."

"Good. Then rock on, bro." Nick urged his horse forward and got back into line ahead of them.

Gabe wasn't sure what *rock on* meant in this context. Nick had found himself a woman, one he'd no doubt marry some day. Maybe he thought his two brothers should do the same.

Gabe wasn't thinking that way himself. He was enjoying competing too much, and that wasn't the kind of life he envisioned leading as a family man. One of these days, maybe after Top Drawer made the Hall of Fame, he'd retire from the circuit, but for now he still loved the challenge.

Sure, he'd been temporarily sidelined by Jack's penny-pinching, but Gabe wouldn't allow his brother to deny him permanently and rob Top Drawer of his chance to shine. They'd work something out. Gabe believed his dad would have wanted him to continue competing, especially with Top Drawer getting closer to that milestone.

In the meantime, though, Gabe was here and so was Morgan. He admitted that he found her sexy. Each time she tossed out that candy her breasts quivered. He couldn't help noticing the fit of her jeans, either. Yeah, if given the chance, he'd be more than willing to get cozy with Morgan.

She seemed to like him okay, too. They could have some adult-rated fun together until he managed to convince Jack to send him back out on the circuit. As long as Morgan didn't expect wedding bells, the two of them could have a *lot* of fun.

3

THROWING OUT candy toward the end of the parade route lifted Morgan's spirits considerably. At the other end of town another field had been designated as the gathering point for participants. Those who were on foot dispersed. Morgan noticed a large horse trailer with the distinctive intertwined *L* and *C* parked on the far side of the field.

Jack led their group toward the trailer, and because Morgan was on Gabe's horse, she had to go along. Then she saw another trailer, considerably less elegant, from the stable where she'd rented Geronimo. The owners had agreed to meet her at the end of the parade. Belatedly she wondered if she'd have any liability for letting someone else ride the horse.

She looked over at Gabe. "How should we work this?"

"Simple. I'll turn in your horse and you turn in mine."

"If they ask you any questions about why—"

"I'll tell them Geronimo needed a more experienced

rider in a parade situation. They should be made aware of that."

"Great. Thanks." Morgan wondered what it would be like to feel so sure of yourself all the time. She never had, although she'd learned to put up a good front. Maybe, when she'd created a solid situation here in Shoshone, she'd feel more grounded.

Until then, she was in fake-it-till-you-make-it territory.

She headed over to the Last Chance trailer. At least she understood now why Sarah and Jack hadn't been as warm as she might have hoped. They thought she'd try to talk them into selling their beloved ranch.

Her wayward shirt had behaved so far, mostly because she'd learned to breathe more shallowly. She kept up that program as she rode Top Drawer over to the trailer, where Jack had dismounted and was organizing the reloading operation.

He glanced up as she approached.

"Gabe asked me to bring Top Drawer here," she said.

"All right. Thanks." Jack's tone was businesslike.

"I'll just get off him and he's all yours."

"That's fine." Jack's dark gaze gave nothing away as he turned to help his mother off her horse.

Looping her purse strap over her shoulder, Morgan prepared to dismount. Whew, the ground was really far away.

Gabe had shortened the stirrups for her, which had helped while she was riding, but now that she had to get off, she had a longer drop to the ground. She managed as best she could, but sure enough, her shirt popped open again.

Once she got back to town, she'd detour past her house—a block off Main Street—and change out of this blasted shirt. She wasn't about to struggle with it for the rest of the day.

As she tried to refasten it quickly, Jack appeared at her elbow. "Just so you know, no part of the Last Chance is for sale. And I mean no part, not even the acreage closest to the road."

Her fingers still gripping the two parts of the snap, Morgan looked up. "I have no designs on your ranch," she said. "I realize you've been plagued by real estate agents eager to make a buck, but that's not me."

His expression didn't soften. "I'm hoping that's true. But it is your job to sell property, so logically the ranch would look like an opportunity."

"Perhaps, but I have no plans in that direction."

Jack's gaze flicked to the other side of the field where Gabe was talking to the owners of the riding stable. "Just so you know, getting chummy with one of the Chance boys won't make any difference."

"I beg your pardon?" The combination of Irish temper and Italian fire was starting to create a burning sensation in her gut.

"Shoshone's a small town, and 'most everyone knows that Gabe prefers a certain…physical attribute in a woman."

"Oh?" As Morgan held her shirt together, flames of fury danced through her system.

"I'd hate to think that you were using that weakness of Gabe's to your advantage."

The fury erupted. "Are we talking about my breasts, Mr. Chance?"

He had the decency to flush. "I'm just worried about—"

"Well, don't trouble yourself for another second! I realize this is a difficult time for your family, and because I respect all that the Chance legacy stands for in this town, I won't tell you exactly what I think of your crude insinuations."

"Listen, I—"

"No, *you* listen." Her voice quivered with rage. "Gabe did me a favor so that I could ride in the parade, and I'm extremely grateful. Please let him know how much that means to me."

Jack looked a little disoriented, as if the conversation had taken a turn he hadn't been prepared for. "Uh, you can tell him yourself when he comes back."

"I'm afraid I can't. My breasts and I don't want to cause either you or your family greater distress, so we're leaving." Ah, the pleasure of turning on her heel and striding away. She had to hold her shirt together because she still hadn't managed to fasten the snap, but even so, it was a most excellent exit.

TALKING WITH the cowboy from the riding stable took longer than Gabe had anticipated, but finally he headed back over toward the Last Chance trailer to find Morgan. The watermelon-eating contest was scheduled to start in thirty minutes, and he had a feeling she'd want to take part. After that would come the sack race, if the activities followed the traditional schedule, and then the hot-dog roast.

Gabe had been a teenager when he'd last taken part in Shoshone's Fourth of July celebration, and he discovered to his surprise that he was looking forward to the day's events once again. Morgan had a lot to do with that. Her excitement was catching. He wanted to spend the day with her and experience Shoshone through her eyes.

Jack was loading his black-and-white paint Bandit into the trailer, and everyone else seemed to have left. Gabe didn't see Morgan anywhere. He hadn't specifically asked her to wait for him, but he'd thought she would. Taking off without saying a word didn't seem like something she'd do. True, he didn't know her all that well, but he had a tough time imagining her being so rude.

Walking to the back of the trailer, Gabe asked Jack if he'd seen Morgan.

"Yeah." Jack closed up the trailer and turned to Gabe. "She said to tell you she appreciated what you'd done for her."

"That's it?"

"Pretty much."

Something was going on. Gabe could feel it, even though Jack was very good at hiding his emotions. "So, she didn't mention where she'd be after this, didn't ask me to meet her somewhere in town?"

"Nope."

"Maybe she left her cell number."

"Nope."

"Damn it, Jack, this smells fishy. She's not the kind of person to leave a message and walk off. I loaned her my *horse*."

"Not the wisest move you've ever made."

Gabe went on alert. "You said something to her, didn't you?"

"I told her we're not selling any part of the Last Chance, if that's what you mean."

"Yeah, well, she knows that, and she's not interested, anyway." Gabe didn't believe for a minute that was the sum total of their conversation. "What else did you say to her?"

Jack blew out a breath. "Look, I realize she's exactly the kind of woman you go for, but—"

"Because she's stacked."

"Well, yeah. And don't tell me she isn't out to capitalize on that. All you have to do is look at her shirt."

"The company that stitched it sent her the wrong size."

"So she says."

"You're calling her a liar?" Gabe stared at his brother in disbelief. "What in hell gives you the right to pass that kind of judgment on a person you don't even know?"

"Common sense! The Last Chance is a real estate goldmine. She's in real estate. Do you really believe she wouldn't like to have a piece of the action?"

"There's no action to have a piece of!"

"She might figure getting horizontal with you could change that."

Gabe pointed a finger at him. "You accused her of having ulterior motives, didn't you?"

Jack shrugged. "I only suggested that—"

"You son of a bitch. I'd punch you in the nose, except for two things. I need to find Morgan and I don't want

Mom to know we had a fight." Gabe turned and left before his temper got the best of him.

Punching Jack would feel great, but it would cause more problems than it would solve. Jack would probably punch back, and Gabe needed his face to be in working order today. He had watermelon and hot dogs to eat. Later on, if he could repair the damage his brother had done, he might even have some kissing to do.

Gabe wasn't a big fan of walking, but he wasn't about to ask Jack to take him into town on his way back to the ranch. Fortunately he was less than a mile from the center of town. Shoshone didn't have a square like some small towns, so everything happened along Main Street. Traditionally one block was closed off on the Fourth. Gabe hoped he'd find Morgan there.

As he neared the roped-off area, he spotted a crowd gathered near a long table covered with butcher paper. Ten folding chairs lined one side. Gabe knew he'd found the site of the watermelon-eating contest. He just had to hope that his instincts were right and Morgan would have come here.

The country band from Spirits and Spurs had set up in a makeshift bandstand near the watermelon contest, and a few people were two-stepping on the asphalt. Red, white and blue banners and crepe paper hung from windows and doorways all along the street and every business was flying a flag. Kids with squirt guns chased each other through the crowd.

Gabe looked for Morgan, but a quick glance around told him she wasn't in the immediate vicinity. With her bright-red hair, he'd spot her immediately. If Jack had ruined this day for her, Gabe might have to go back to the ranch and pound on his brother, after all.

Then he saw her over by the Shoshone Diner, where Madge and Edgar Perkins were distributing plastic bibs advertising their business. Apparently they were still sponsoring the contest, as they'd done for as long as Gabe could remember. He'd never paid much attention to that kind of comforting stability, but after talking with Morgan, he had a new appreciation for it.

As Morgan tied on her bib, Gabe noticed that she was wearing a baggy T-shirt instead of her satin Western shirt. She might have decided to change clothes because of the snap issue, but he could also believe Jack's comments might have had something to do with it. His older brother had a lot to answer for.

Adjusting the brim of his gray Stetson, Gabe walked over to the diner. Morgan was laughing at something Edgar had said and obviously hadn't spotted him yet.

"Hey, Gabe!" Madge called out. "Come on over here and get a bib. You were always real good at this."

Morgan's head came up with a start, and the happy laughter faded as she looked in Gabe's direction. Her body stiffened and she clenched her jaw.

Yep, Jack would pay for this. "You bet I'll take a bib, Mrs. Perkins." Gabe accepted the piece of plastic and tied the ends around his neck. "Hi there, Morgan."

"Hi, Gabe."

"Say, weren't you two riding together in the parade a while ago?" Madge asked.

"Yes." Morgan turned to her. "Gabe was nice enough to switch horses with me. His was better trained than mine, and I'm not a very good rider."

"You had a very stubborn horse," Gabe said.

"Yes, well." She swallowed. "Did you happen to talk to Jack?"

"I did, as a matter of fact. I gather you talked to him, too."

"Yes. We had a...conversation." Her expression was carefully controlled.

"You two can catch up later," Edgar said. "It's time to eat us some watermelon!" He lifted an old-fashioned school bell and started ringing it. "Watermelon-eating contest! Last chance to enter!"

Morgan reached for the ties around her neck. "You know what? I don't think I'll do this, after all."

Gabe caught both her hands in his. "Don't you dare chicken out on me, Morgan O'Connelli." He hadn't counted on her hands being quite so soft and warm. Or her mouth being quite so close and inviting.

She glanced up at him. "Gabe, it's not a good idea." Her eyes darkened as they had when he'd chased down Geronimo.

He didn't think fear was the reason this time. He'd bet good money she was as sexually aware of him as he was of her. As further evidence, pink tinged her cheeks and her breathing changed.

"Go on, both of you." Madge shooed them toward the table as if they were five-year-olds, and Gabe was forced to let go of Morgan.

She allowed herself to be herded toward the table, but fumbled with the ties of her bib along the way. "Seriously, I'm taking myself out of the competition."

"That's exactly the problem," Madge shot back. "There's too much seriousness these days. It does people good to act foolish once in a while. Sit right there, Morgan. Gabe, you take the next seat."

Gabe sat down and glanced over at Morgan with a shrug. "I think you're outvoted."

"All right." Morgan met his gaze and a flicker of her usual good humor returned. "But I need to warn you, I've been looking forward to these events for a long time, and when it comes to watermelon contests, I eat to win."

Gabe smiled. "Them's fighting words, ma'am."

Madge put a hand on each of their shoulders. "Morgan, it's only fair to tell you that when Gabe was in high school he won this competition three years out of four."

"Because one year I beat his ass." Nick clapped Gabe on the back and sat down next to him. "You're toast, bro. I've been practicing."

"So that explains the love handles!" Gabe had never been so glad to see Nick in his life. Maybe Nick's cheerful acceptance of Morgan would erase the bad impression Jack had left.

"A guy has to do what a guy has to do." Nick leaned around Gabe to talk to Morgan. "Watch out for my brother. He cheats."

"I do not!" Gabe looked at Morgan and was gratified to see a smile back on her face. "Don't listen to him. It's character assassination, pure and simple. Nick's the sneaky brother."

"I'll vouch for that." Aiming her camera at the two men, Dominique crouched in front of the table and took a shot. "Nick is very sneaky. I found this taped to my lens cap an hour ago." She waggled the ring finger of her left hand, where a diamond caught the sunlight.

"Hey, hey, hey!" Gabe left his seat and came around the table. "Could we have a short delay in the proceedings? My brother Nick just had the good sense to propose to Dominique."

"And I had the good sense to accept," Dominique said.

Gabe hugged her. "Welcome to the family. Nick's a lucky guy."

Nick joined them on the other side of the table and put an arm around his fiancée. "Grandpa Archie used to say that Chance men are lucky when it counts."

"Nice going, Nick." Gabe shook Nick's hand as the rest of the people at the table and in the surrounding crowd came up to offer their congratulations.

Morgan joined in as naturally as if she'd lived in Shoshone for years. Gabe liked seeing her relax back into her normal upbeat personality. Best of all, he didn't detect any envy or wistfulness on her part. No engagement fever going on, there. She probably wanted to keep focused on her career, and that was a good thing.

At last Edgar Perkins rang the school bell again. "This is all very exciting, but we're falling behind schedule. I need the contestants to be seated so we can bring out the watermelon."

Gabe watched Morgan to make sure she didn't use this interruption to sneak out, but she hurried back to her chair beside him.

Once Nick sat down, Gabe leaned toward him. "Does Mom know about this?"

"Yeah, and Jack and Emmett and Mary Lou. You

would've, too, but you were over dealing with the Appaloosa."

"Must've been a pretty quiet announcement. I didn't hear any commotion over there."

"It was a quietly emotional announcement, not a wild and crazy one. Mom's feeling kind of teary today, anyway, and this started up the waterworks again. You know how Jack gets when she cries."

Gabe's gut tightened. "Speaking of Jack, I—"

"Here are your watermelon wedges, ladies and gents." Edgar came over with two plates and Madge followed with two more. On each plate sat a quarter of a melon sliced lengthwise. The process was repeated until all ten contestants had watermelon.

"We'll talk," Nick said. "But not now."

"Nope, not now." Gabe tucked his Stetson under his chair before giving Nick and then Morgan the evil eye. "I hope you both know you're going down."

Excitement sparkled in Morgan's blue-green gaze. "We'll just see about that, Gabe Chance." Pulling a scrunchie out of her pocket, she tied back her hair. "I intend to chomp my way to victory."

Now that was the Morgan he liked to see—full of piss and vinegar. He thought again about that Italian mother of hers. This could be a very interesting day, and quite possibly a more interesting night.

4

WHEN MORGAN had heard about the watermelon-eating contest a week ago, she'd decided to sign up for it, as well as any other activity going on during the celebration. She'd always enjoyed contests, but her parents frowned on competition. Besides, their wanderlust had pretty much guaranteed Morgan wouldn't be playing organized sports.

Watermelon-eating wasn't exactly a sport, but she would take what she could get, although she hadn't expected to be squaring off against the Chance brothers. Somewhere she'd heard that a woman had to be careful of a man's ego and not beat him at games. Forget that noise. As long as she was here, she planned to whip everyone at this table, including the gorgeous Gabe Chance.

Edgar Perkins raised his hand. "The rules are that you may not hold on to the plate. You can touch it to pull it closer, but you may not hold on. Anyone caught holding the plate will be disqualified. We'll start on my signal."

Morgan's blood was up. After her set-to with Jack

she'd headed to town ready to show everyone this girl knew how to have a good time. She'd changed her shirt because it was a pain in the ass having to worry about that snap, but otherwise, she intended to enjoy herself fully.

Then Gabe had appeared, and her bravado had disappeared. His family didn't like her, so she'd decided she didn't like them, either, and that had to include Gabe. No doubt he'd choose pleasing his family over pleasing her, so why bother with him? She'd only set herself up for heartbreak.

Madge Perkins hadn't made it easy to duck out, though, and now Morgan had recommitted herself to the contest and to a day of fun. Gabe's mother and his oldest brother weren't around, so if he wanted to share that day with her, she wouldn't push him away. It was a free country—which was what they were celebrating—after all.

"On my signal," said Edgar. "Ready, set, go!"

Morgan dove in. She ate without stopping, swallowing pieces whole and biting off gigantic chunks of the sweet melon. She swallowed her share of seeds in the process.

She might be sick after this, but she didn't care. Watermelon juice coated her mouth and her chin. As she buried her face deep in the cool pulp, even her cheeks became slicked with pink slime.

She paid no attention to Gabe, chomping away on his melon next to her. Focus was the name of the game. But even through her intense concentration she heard people starting to chant her name. Dominique was pulling for Nick, of course. All the other contestants, including

Gabe, had cheering sections. But Morgan didn't know many people, so if they were shouting her name, she must be ahead.

She ate faster and realized Edgar was leaning close, watching her and Gabe intently. She was down to the white part when he sang out "winner!" Looking up, she discovered Edgar's hand poised over her head. She'd done it.

"Congratulations, champ."

She turned, her chin dripping with juice, to find Gabe in the same condition, and he was grinning at her.

"You did it." He didn't sound upset. He even seemed happy that she'd won. Then he did the most amazing thing. He put his hand behind her head, pulled her close, and kissed her, watermelon juice and all.

A cheer went up from the crowd.

Morgan was too shocked to react at first. Gabe was kissing her? In public? When they were both totally slimed with watermelon juice?

Then the heat of his kiss began to register. He was using his tongue. And so was she. Watermelon juice made for one sexy kissing session.

She forgot where they were. She forgot to breathe. She forgot her name. Whistling and stomping noises caused her to realize vaguely that their behavior wasn't particularly appropriate for this venue. Even so, she had the urge to pull Gabe under the table and continue the kiss a long time.

Mercifully, he drew back before she did something really embarrassing. A low chuckle rich with implications told her that he'd been a little surprised by the intensity, too. "We might want to try that again some-time," he murmured.

She lifted heavy-lidded eyes to his. "I'm game."

"So I gathered."

Edgar approached with the prize, which was a gift certificate for two lunches at the Shoshone Diner. "Well, Gabe, you are sure a good loser. I don't think I've ever seen such a good loser in my life."

"No kidding," Nick said. "Good thing I didn't win. I don't think I could have handled playing tonsil hockey with my brother."

Dominique walked forward. "Wanna see the pics?"

"You took pictures?" Morgan wasn't so sure about that.

"Get used to it," Nick said. "Dominique takes pictures of *everything*. Don't be surprised if this ends up in a gallery in Jackson, although I promise she'll ask first."

"Don't worry," Dominique said. "Just say the word and I'll delete it. But I hope you don't tell me to, because I think it's great." She turned the camera so that Morgan could see the shot on the back screen.

There she was, kissing Gabe for all she was worth. Good thing he was kissing her for all he was worth, too, or she'd have been mortified. As it was, she was sort of…fascinated. She'd never seen a picture of herself kissing anyone, let alone a hottie like Gabe Chance. She couldn't look away. The photo captured exactly what she'd been feeling—wonder, passion, discovery.

"I want a copy," Gabe said.

She stared at him. "You do?"

"Yeah." He smiled at her. "Wouldn't you like one, too? To commemorate winning the watermelon-eating contest?"

"Maybe." She thought about it. "But what would you be commemorating?"

His gaze was open and his voice rang with sincerity. "Our first kiss."

A chorus of *awww* went up from the crowd.

Morgan felt as if someone had poured warm syrup in the general area of her heart. She couldn't remember any guy saying something that sweet to her. She studied Gabe to make sure he wasn't poking fun, but she saw no evidence that he was.

"I'll be happy to get each of you copies," Dominique said. "But how would you feel about me turning it into a gallery shot?"

Gabe shrugged. "It's okay with me."

Morgan wondered if he'd thought about potential consequences. "Maybe you should check with your family first."

Gabe didn't hesitate. "It's none of their business."

"That's the spirit." Nick pushed back his chair and accepted one of the wipe cloths Madge handed to each of the contestants. "Maintaining the Chance family reputation has been highly overrated, wouldn't you say, little brother?"

"That's for sure, big brother." From his tone of voice, Gabe seemed to be making more than a casual remark.

Morgan recognized the kind of unspoken communication that happened between siblings. She and her brothers and sisters, all seven of them, shared certain truths that could only come from weathering a common past. From the look that passed between Nick and Gabe, she gathered that both of them had some problems with what had happened in that shared past. Well, join the club.

"Sack races in fifteen minutes!" shouted someone from the door of the Shoshone Feed Store. "Come collect your sacks if you're gonna be in it!"

"That's me," Gabe said. "Morgan, are you up for this?"

She grinned at him. "You couldn't keep me away."

"I was hoping you'd say that. Nick? You racing?"

"Yes, he is," said Dominique. "I made him promise to be in everything so I could take pictures."

Nick groaned. "Pictures that will be used against me when we have kids."

"And grandkids!" Dominique said, laughing.

Morgan listened without a smidgen of envy. As the oldest in a large family, she'd grown up taking care of her brothers and sisters and in many cases sacrificing her own needs to theirs. She wouldn't mind hooking up with someone for fun and games, but she wanted to enjoy her freedom a while longer. The idea of having kids didn't excite her at all.

GABE HADN'T MINDED losing the watermelon-eating contest, but the sack race was going to be all his. When he crossed the finish line only a foot ahead of Morgan, he claimed a victory kiss. Games that ended in kissing Morgan were a good thing.

Hanging out with Morgan, Nick and Dominique was a good thing, too. If Morgan hadn't been there, Gabe might have felt like a fifth wheel tagging along after Nick and Dominique. A foursome was better, and they made up their own team for events like the spoon-and-egg relay.

Gabe couldn't remember the last time he'd had such a pressure-free day. Sure, he played the games to win, but when he didn't win, he could still dream up an excuse to kiss Morgan. Kissing Morgan beat winning all to hell.

Late in the afternoon the four of them helped Josie, owner of Spirits and Spurs, carry her tables outside. Traditionally Shoshone's Fourth of July ended with a street dance, and Josie was no fool. She'd figured out that serving food and drinks in the open air made a lot more sense than trying to coax people into the saloon.

She rewarded the four of them with bottles of beer and a prime table next to the section of street where the dancing would take place. Once they were settled, Morgan and Dominique left to repair their hair and makeup in the saloon's bathroom.

That presented Gabe with his first chance to talk with Nick alone. He might not have another one, so he latched onto it. Taking a pull on his beer, he glanced over at Nick. "Jack's getting out of hand."

"He's been out of hand for a while now. Demanding that you stop competing is only the latest stunt in a long line of weirdness."

"I'm gonna find a way to compete so Top Drawer can make the Hall of Fame."

Nick picked at the label on his beer bottle. "I know you are. And you should." He glanced up. "Of the three of us, you have the most right to be out there representing the family, and Top Drawer deserves his shot."

"Let's not start that half-brother shit again. As far as I'm concerned, we're all just brothers." Gabe had never felt any differently, but convincing Jack and Nick was an uphill battle.

Jack's mother had left the ranch and her marriage when Jack was a toddler. Despite Sarah's continued requests, Jack had never called her Mom, as if he felt obligated to make the distinction that he was her stepson.

Nick and Gabe had both thought they were Sarah's kids, but just recently Nick had found a document proving that Sarah wasn't his biological mother, either. Instead he was the result of an affair his father had had prior to meeting Sarah. Nick's mother had died, and Nick had come to the ranch as a baby. His father and Sarah had never told him the truth, and the community had helped keep their secret.

That left Gabe as the only son born to Jonathan and Sarah. Three sons, three different mothers. It made no difference to Gabe. In fact, he was determined to hang on to a sense of unity, even though Jack was currently behaving like an ass. But Nick and Jack weren't so dedicated to the concept. Jack was the most stubborn about it, but Nick had his moments. Like now.

"Dad had a special feeling for you," Nick said. "That's why he encouraged you to get into the cutting-horse competition in the first place."

"He had a special feeling for all of us. You know damned well he didn't play favorites. He was busting his buttons over you becoming a large-animal vet."

"Nah, that wasn't the same. My degree isn't exciting.

You winning ribbons and trophies and then getting prize money on top of it—that's exciting. He got a vicarious thrill out of you being out there."

Gabe considered that as he took another swig of his beer. "Is there any chance Jack is jealous of how Dad felt about me competing and that's why he wants to shut me down?"

Nick shook his head. "Don't think so. Jack's never seemed jealous of either of us. I think he's always cherished his position as first-born. But, dear God, is he turning into an anal son of a bitch! All he thinks about is the bottom line, preserving the ranch exactly as Dad left it. He's taking his responsibility way too seriously."

Gabe sighed. "Yeah, well, guilt is a powerful thing."

"And so stupid! That rollover was all Dad's fault. He should have waited for better weather or until Jack was available to go fetch that horse."

"What horse?" Morgan asked as the women returned to the table and took their seats.

"Nothing," Gabe said. "You know cowboys. Always talking about some horse or other."

Morgan didn't pursue it. Gabe liked that about her. She was interested in things without being nosy. He hadn't had time to tell Nick about Jack's treatment of Morgan, but maybe that should stay between him and Jack, anyway.

Gabe didn't know for sure where this new friendship with Morgan was headed, but every time he looked at her, he thought of mixing it up on some rumpled bedsheets. More important, he didn't see white lace and promises, so whether Jack ever warmed to Morgan might not matter.

What a great day they'd had, though. Night was settling in, soft and mild, and the mosquitoes hadn't been bad at all. Gabe looked forward to dancing with Morgan and having a reason to hold her close. In the meantime, they'd drink beer and eat some of Josie's food, probably hamburgers. It was that kind of night.

"You know what?" Morgan's eyes shone with excitement. "Dominique just told me about the ghosts that supposedly hang out in the bar. I want to help carry the furniture back in when Josie locks up so I can see if any come around tonight. Fourth of July seems like a prime time to me."

Gabe chuckled. "There're no ghosts. Josie came up with a marketing angle and she's playing it for all it's worth, even renaming the place Spirits and Spurs. I gotta hand it to her."

"Aw." Morgan looked disappointed. "I was all set to see some—what was the name you used, Dominique?"

"Nick said they were called Ghost Drinkers in the Bar."

"Yeah." Morgan grinned. "Like Ghost Riders in the Sky. I still want to help put everything away tonight. Josie might be making it up or she might not. How old is this place, anyway?"

"Josie knows for sure," Nick said. "But it's seventy-five or eighty years old, at least. It was already here when Grandpa Archie and Grandma Nelsie moved to Shoshone, although it was called the Rusty Spur then."

"Our great-uncle Seth, Grandma Nelsie's brother, married the woman who owned it," Gabe added, "but later on they moved down to Arizona. Their kids and grandkids are still down there but they come up to the Last Chance once in a while."

"And the Chance family all stayed here," Morgan said. "It must be cool to live in the same place where your grandparents settled."

"Well, it is," Gabe said, "unless you get so stuck in the past and tradition that you can't move forward." He was thinking of Jack and wondered if Morgan would figure that out. She was a smart lady.

"You're right," Nick said. "I'll bet Grandpa Archie wasn't a fan of rigid thinking when it came to the ranch. I'm pretty sure Dad told me that switching from cattle to horses was Archie's idea, but he didn't live to see it happen."

Morgan gazed at both of them. "Was your Grandpa Archie a drinking man?"

Gabe nodded. "Not to excess, and I was pretty young when he died, but from what I've heard, he enjoyed a shot of whiskey now and then."

"Yes, definitely," Nick said. "I remember Dad saying Archie took it neat."

"Would he have ordered whiskey in this bar?" Morgan pointed to the doorway.

"I think so," Gabe said. "Jack used to talk about Archie going to the Rusty Spur while Nelsie was shopping. Archie wasn't big on shopping, so he had to fortify himself."

Nick raised his beer bottle in agreement. "I remember Jack saying that, too. For sure Grandpa would have come here for a drink back when his brother-in-law was part owner." He looked at Morgan. "Why are you asking?"

Morgan looked pleased with herself. "Because if he did, and Josie's not making up the ghost part, then you two could go in there tonight and ask his opinion about the future of the ranch."

Gabe didn't believe in ghosts, and no way did he want to spend the night in a deserted bar with his brother. But if Morgan was game, he was more than ready to play along. Hanging out with her in a darkened tavern wasn't a bad idea at all. "There aren't any ghosts," he said, "but if you want to see for yourself, I'm in. I'll bet Josie would give us the key and let us lock up after ourselves."

"There's only one problem with the plan, bro." Nick glanced over at Dominique. "We're planning to take off about ten, and there's no way Josie will close up that early."

"You two don't have to stay," Gabe said. In fact, he hoped they wouldn't. He'd already pictured how cozy that tavern could be with only him and Morgan inside.

"But I'm your ride home."

"Don't worry about that," Morgan said immediately. "I can drive Gabe back to the ranch later on. It's not far."

"That would be great." Gabe loved the way this was shaping up. The evening was open-ended, which left room for all sorts of interesting developments.

5

A VAGABOND LIFE did teach a girl to be spontaneous. Morgan might prefer a more planned existence than the one in which she'd grown up, but she could go with the flow when necessary. Or desirable, as was the case with this ghost caper.

The minute Dominique had told Morgan about the possibility of ghosts in the bar, Morgan had wanted an excuse to check it out. Gabe and Nick had conveniently provided it, although both of them claimed not to believe in ghosts. Morgan was neither a believer nor a non-believer. She just thought people should be open to new experiences.

And now, five hours after she'd first concocted this scheme, she and Gabe were sitting in near-darkness, one lone neon Budweiser sign for light. They had only a six-pack and each other for company. Well, unless the Ghost Drinkers in the Bar showed up.

Josie, a tall blonde who wore her hair in a single braid down her back, had been good-natured about the whole thing. She'd given them a key to lock up when they were done and had shown them the mail slot where they could drop it back inside on the floor. She'd also promised them free drinks the following night if they saw or heard ghosts and were willing to testify to the fact.

The room smelled of cigarette smoke and beer, not what Morgan usually associated with sexual fantasies. And yet…there was something illicit and subtly romantic about being alone in this bar after closing with a man as potent as Gabe Chance. Even without a ghostly presence, the room vibrated with energy just because Gabe was there.

She had to pinch herself to make sure she wasn't dreaming. Except for her exchange with Jack, today had been perfect, and now she had her high-school crush sitting next to her in the dark. Speaking of paranormal occurrences, she just might levitate.

"I told you there were no ghosts." Gabe opened a beer for each of them and set them on the table. "Josie created the rumor for publicity purposes. She's hoping we'll claim to see ghosts so we can get a couple of free drinks."

"I don't think so." Morgan sipped the tart beer and put the can back on the table. "She knows you, and she's beginning to know me. She wouldn't expect either of us to create a lie for the sake of free drinks."

"Then maybe she thinks we won't be able to resist making up a good story just for the entertainment value."

"That makes no sense, either, Gabe. I'm trying to get a real estate business going and you're a Chance, for God's sake. Chance men don't lie about things like ghosts for personal gain or to entertain their buddies. You have more honor than to do something like that."

Gabe's soft laughter tickled her nerve endings. "You may have an exaggerated idea of how noble Chance men are."

"You're not noble?" Her chair was right next to his, and they'd positioned themselves so they faced the small stage where the country band usually played. For some reason Morgan had thought the ghosts, if they arrived, might want to appear on stage.

Gabe took off his Stetson and laid it on the table before sliding an arm around her shoulders. "Not all that noble. I had an ulterior motive for agreeing to this ghost hunt."

"And what would that be?" She resisted the impulse to snuggle against him and telegraph her eagerness. He might have been her fantasy man for years, but that was her secret.

"Getting you alone in a dark room."

She glanced over at him and allowed herself to flirt a little. "What if I said that I thought the same thing?"

His fingers traced a circular pattern on her upper arm. "Then I'd have to wonder why we're sitting here waiting for ghosts when we could be doing something more…satisfying."

Her heart kicked into high gear. She loved knowing that he wanted her. "Couldn't we multi-task? Keep an eye out for ghosts while we explore other options?"

Pulling her closer, he cupped her cheek in his free hand. "Not if I'm doing it right."

Whew. That was the answer of a self-assured man. She could have predicted that he'd be confident, but experiencing that confidence first-hand thrilled her. All her interest in the paranormal vanished. If the ghosts showed up, they'd have to amuse themselves. Gabe Chance was about to kiss her, and that took precedence over everything else.

His mouth hovered nearer. "This reminds me of sitting in the back row of the movie theater or in a parked car. Same awkward angle."

"Same agonizing anticipation." She tried to be cool, tried to breathe normally, but it was a losing battle. Although she'd kissed Gabe several times today, they'd always had an audience, a built-in braking system. Now they had none.

Gabe brushed his lips against hers. "We could improve on this position."

"You're right." Refusing to worry about whether he would think she was too aggressive, she left her chair and crawled into his lap.

"Better?" Sitting astride him, she had no doubt what he was thinking about. The evidence formed a hot bulge that nestled conveniently between her thighs. Knowing that she'd caused that reaction sent her pulse racing and her spirits soaring.

He groaned. "Depends on your definition of *better.* The angle's nice, but the temptation is worse."

She wrapped her arms around his neck and leaned forward to nibble on his lower lip. His obvious desire gave her the courage to be the siren she'd always longed to be, especially with him. "Face it, Gabe. You didn't come in here to resist temptation."

"No." He gathered the hem of her T-shirt in both hands. "I want all the temptation I can get."

"Then I'm guessing you want my shirt off."

"Among other things."

Quivering with excitement, she leaned back and raised her arms over her head. "Then go for it, Mr. Chance."

He pulled her shirt over her head and tossed it on the table. "Damn, now I wish we had more light than a neon beer sign."

"I don't. The windows face the street." Arching her back, she reached for her bra hooks. She had big girls, and big girls needed at least four hooks. She couldn't expect Gabe to navigate through all those.

"True." His voice sounded raspy, as if he might be having a little trouble with his breathing, too.

"Besides, light would scare away the ghosts." She took off her bra and threw it in the general direction of the table.

He gulped. "At this moment, I don't give a flying fig if Casper and all his friends show up. You are magnificent, woman." Yet he didn't grab, didn't even reach for her at all, as if waiting to be invited.

Cupping her breasts, she gazed into his shadowy face. "Your brother accused me of using these assets to further my goal of Chance family domination. He told me you had a certain weakness."

Gabe drew an unsteady breath. "He's right. I've been dreaming about touching you ever since that snap popped open."

"Yet you're holding back."

"I'm…I'm afraid once I touch you, there won't be any stopping."

Disappointment shot through her. "And you didn't

come prepared." She certainly hadn't. Zipping home to pick up condoms had seemed like an assumption she shouldn't make, almost as if she'd be tempting fate and pinning her hopes on something out of reach.

"I didn't come prepared."

"Oh." Feeling like a fool, she let her arms drop to her sides.

He cleared his throat. "But the men's room here is always prepared. I, um, made a purchase the last time I went in there."

"Oh."

"So if you—"

"Gabe Chance, if you don't touch me right now, I'm going to combust."

With a groan of pure delight, he cupped her breasts in both hands. "Damn, you feel good."

"So do you." She closed her eyes to better enjoy the sweet sensation of his callused hands stroking, kneading, caressing, as if he knew exactly what she craved. Against all logic, she'd known it could be like this with Gabe.

His breathing grew more labored as he rubbed his thumbs over her nipples. "Your skin is so soft. My hands are rough from—"

"I like that." Bracing her hands on his knees, she arched into his caress. "I like knowing you have hard-working hands."

"You're giving them one hell of a vacation."

"Good." Her booted feet located the rungs of the chair to give her stability. Having a dream come true made her bold. "Your mouth deserves one, too." Moving her hands to his shoulders, she lifted herself from his lap so that she was in the perfect position for him to…oh, yeah. Gabe knew how to make use of that position.

As he licked and sucked, murmuring words of praise for the bounty she was providing, her womb tightened. She'd known from that first watermelon kiss that she'd been right years ago. This was a man who had the power to drive her crazy.

And she needed more than his mouth at her breasts. She needed release, and it wasn't far away, if only she could get back to where… Slowly she lowered herself into his lap and gave him a tongue-worthy kiss to make up for taking away all that oral gratification. At least he still had his hands full.

Gripping his knees again, she pushed her hips forward and wedged her sweet spot intimately against the erection straining the denim of his jeans. Then she let her head fall back and rocked forward against that tantalizing bulge. "Mmm."

He gasped. "Morgan…"

"What, Gabe?" Heart racing, she wiggled a fraction closer. "Am I hurting you?"

"Good God, no. But I—"

"Just let me…" Right there. She didn't even have to move much, if she could just press against him for a moment longer… Her pulse hammered as the quickening began. Almost there. She struggled for breath. "Pinch…my nipples."

He did, and she felt the first spasm. She whimpered and rocked against him. "Again."

He squeezed once, twice, and she gasped as the trembling began in earnest. "Oh, yes. *Yes.*" Gripping his knees, she pushed hard against that rigid denim as her body quaked in response to the glorious pressure. She clenched her jaw to keep from crying out.

Her climax left her limp and panting. She slumped forward. "Thank...you."

"Oh, Morgan." Cradling her face in both hands, he covered her with kisses. "You're incredible, and I need you so much. I need you *now*."

"Yes... I know..." In her dazed state, she wasn't sure how to make that happen. They had no bed, and the floor didn't seem like a good idea.

But apparently a serious case of lust inspired Gabe to improvise. He lifted her onto the round table and made short work of her boots, jeans and soaked panties. He didn't bother taking off his own clothes. Through heavy-lidded eyes she watched him unbuckle his belt and jerk down his zipper. The condom took no time at all.

His breathing ragged, he bracketed her hips and plunged deep. His groan of satisfaction came through clenched teeth, but it spoke volumes about his state of mind, or rather mindlessness.

Instinctively she wrapped her legs around his waist so that she had leverage and could be more than a passenger on this cruise to paradise.

"I'll just hang out here for a minute." He sounded winded, as if he'd run a footrace. "Get my bearings."

Wrapping one hand around his neck, she traced the line of his mouth with her finger. He captured that finger between his teeth, pulled it into his mouth and began to suck.

"Wow. That's...that's nice." She wasn't sure why, but

having him suck rhythmically on her finger while his cock was up to the hilt inside her had almost the same effect as if he were stroking back and forth.

Slowly he released her finger. "God, you're responsive."

"Not always, but tonight…tonight I can't seem to help myself." *Because I'm with you.* "I want it all." She used her free hand to unsnap his shirt. It fell open and she stroked his heaving, sweat-slicked chest. Even the smattering of hair covering his pecs was damp.

He groaned again, and deep inside her vagina his penis twitched. "I'm hanging on by a thread."

Her voice lowered to a soft purr. "Then let go." She began drawing lazy circles around his tight nipples.

"Not yet." Finding her mouth with his, he took her by the shoulders and eased her back on to the table. Then he kissed her deeply as he ran both hands down her arms. In a maneuver straight out of a pirate movie, he laced his fingers through hers and raised her arms over her head, anchoring them to the table.

He was ravishing her. And she loved it.

He lifted his mouth, hovering near, his rapid breathing feathering her wet lips. "I think this is what they call fantasy sex," he murmured.

"X-rated entertainment for the ghosts."

"There are no ghosts." He nuzzled the curve of her neck and placed kisses along her collarbone. "Just one hot woman and one desperate man."

"Desperate?"

"Oh, yeah. I'm right on the edge, but I want to make you come first."

"You did."

"No, *you* did. This one's on me. Let's see if I've learned anything." Closing his mouth around her nipple, he moved his hips a fraction closer, tightening the connection between them. Then he rolled her nipple between his tongue and the roof of his mouth as he pushed forward with his hips. The motion was subtle.

But it was enough. He'd found the exact spot and was applying pressure. And all the while he rolled her nipple against the roof of his mouth with a little more force, and a little more, and yet a little more...

"Oh, Gabe! Kiss me. Kiss me now before I...I'm going to scream!"

He muffled the sound of her cries as her orgasm ripped through her like a flash flood, lifting her hips from the table and sending waves of pleasure shivering through her body.

She was still arched like a bow and trembling when he began to pound into her, his strokes swift and sure, his rhythm picking up speed until he tore his mouth from hers and began to pant. His grip on her hands tightened and he gazed down at her, although his face was in shadow.

She could barely see his eyes, could only faintly make out that a lock of his sandy hair had fallen over his damp forehead. And she, too, wished they had more light.

"So...good...so..." His mouth came down on hers as he drove home once more and his body shuddered.

She absorbed the staccato pulse of his climax with a joyous sense of accomplishment. She'd given him pleasure. No matter what else happened between them—even if nothing did—she would know that in this moment he wouldn't have traded places with anyone in the world. And neither would she.

GABE HAD SUSPECTED from the moment he'd first spied Morgan on Geronimo that she was no ordinary woman. With that cockeyed name and her considerable endowments, she already stood out from the crowd.

But now he had a better idea of what made her so special. She gave a hundred percent in anything she did, and that included—boy, did it ever—having sex. Her Italian mama would be proud.

Releasing his grip on her hands, he cupped her face and gave her a long, gentle kiss. She responded as he would have expected, kissing him back as if she felt the same sense of gratitude he did.

Slowly he ended the kiss and braced his hands on either side of her head. "That...that was the best sex I've ever had in my life."

"I'd have to say the same."

"I guess now we have to decide what we want to do about it."

"Have more?"

He laughed. "Well, yeah, obviously. But we have to decide the when and where part. Are you tired?"

"If you're asking whether I'd choose sleep over sex with you, then you haven't been paying attention."

"Ah, Morgan, you flatter me."

"Ah, Gabe, you turn me on. But we probably shouldn't stay here."

"No."

"I'm thinking my place."

He smiled down at her. "You got any ghosts?"

"Not that I know of, but I do have a box of condoms."

"I'll take condoms over ghosts anyday." With some regret, but with the promise of more happy times very soon, he eased away from her. "I'll make a quick trip to the men's room and be right back."

"I'll put myself back together while you're gone."

"If any ghosts show up, offer them a beer. I don't think we'll need that six-pack, after all." He thought about that as he went to the back to take care of business.

He'd assumed they'd drink at least some of the six-pack as a way to loosen up and get into a fooling-around mood. They'd each had about two sips of the stuff before they were into full make-out mode. He hadn't felt that kind of strong attraction to a woman in a long time.

And the attraction had been followed by world-class sex. Because he wanted to focus on his competition for now—once he sorted things out with Jack—he wasn't interested in tying himself down, but if he were, Morgan would be perfect. Then he had an unsettling thought. She could be thinking the same thing, that they were perfect for each other. And she might not have an aversion to making it permanent.

That meant at some point they'd have to discuss the subject. He'd be completely honest with her and hope she'd offer him the same courtesy. In some ways he wished he'd met her two or three years from now, when he'd reached his goals for himself and Top Drawer.

But he couldn't bring himself to regret what had happened tonight. A guy could go his whole life and not experience that kind of great sex. He was one lucky cowboy.

Turning out the bathroom light, he stepped into the darkened bar and paused to let his eyes adjust so he wouldn't bang into things.

"Gabe?" Her voice sounded a little quivery, as if she might be nervous about something.

"What?" He hoped she wasn't ready to have a talk about where all this might lead.

"I don't know what you're going to think about this…"

He decided to preempt whatever she was trying to say and save her the embarrassment. "Look, Morgan, I loved having sex with you, but I don't want to get serious about anyone right now."

"Me, either! Did you think that's what I was going to say? That I'm husband-hunting?"

"Well…yeah."

"That's the furthest thing from my mind. But I did think I should mention something to you."

He was relieved, but wondered what other bombshell she had to drop. "What's that?"

"I just saw a ghost."

6

FOR A GUY who supposedly didn't believe in ghosts, Gabe rushed her out of the bar so fast they almost forgot to put the key through the mail slot. Morgan had a sneaky suspicion that underneath his manly man pose was a little kid who did believe in ghosts.

"You didn't see a ghost," Gabe insisted as they walked rapidly down Main Street, which was now deserted. He had a firm hold on her hand, as if he didn't trust her to keep heading away from the haunted bar. "Somebody made a U-turn in the street and their headlights shone through the window. That's all it was."

"No, that's not all it was." Morgan had been a little freaked out, but she'd wanted to stay and see what the ghost would do. The shimmery light that had drifted through the locked front door and over to a corner table had definitely not been a car's headlights. "You walked right past it. Didn't you notice anything?"

His answer was delivered in a no-nonsense tone. "No. Didn't see a thing." He walked faster.

"So where are we going now?"

"Your place."

"Okay. But I'm just wondering. Do you know where that is?"

His pace slowed. "Uh, not exactly."

"Didn't think so." She worked hard not to laugh. "We have to go back the other way."

"Oh." He glanced down the street toward Spirits and Spurs. A light fog had drifted in, and the bar looked even spookier than when they'd left.

Gabe shook his finger at it. "I know what happened. Josie set us up. Dollars to doughnuts she has a projection system on a timer, and all she had to do was activate it."

"Then I wish we'd stayed. We could have figured out exactly where that shimmery light was coming from. Now we'll never know for sure."

"I know for sure. It was Josie. Eventually I'll get her to admit it. I'm surprised she'd try something like that, considering."

"Considering what?"

He didn't answer right away, which aroused her curiosity even more. "Is there some unwritten rule that nobody plays tricks on a Chance?"

"Hardly. My dad was always messing with people, and they'd mess with him right back." Gabe pointed toward the feed store. "You see that plastic horse on the porch roof next to the Shoshone Feed Store sign?"

Morgan glanced up at the life-sized statue. "I remember it from when I lived here before, except I thought it was white back then."

"It was white for years. It's also an anatomically correct stallion."

"Huh. I never noticed."

"You would have noticed after my dad snuck in here one dark night and painted the horse's balls blue."

Morgan laughed. "When he was a randy teenager, I'll bet."

"Uh, no. He was fifty-seven going on seventeen. He and Ronald, the feed store owner, were high-school buddies who never grew out of playing tricks on each other. The week before, my dad had walked outside to discover a full-grown male buffalo with a red bow on his head tied to the hitching post beside the barn."

"A gift from Ronald."

"Yep. So the ball-painting was payback. Dad took Jack with him to hold the ladder and keep watch."

"Jack, huh?" Morgan had a tough time imagining the cowboy she'd met playing pranks.

"Oh, yeah. Jack was my dad's right-hand man when it came to stuff like that. But they didn't get along on every front, especially when it came to Josie. My dad didn't like it when Jack hooked up with her."

"Jack and Josie?" That blew Morgan away. Josie loved to laugh and have fun, but Jack didn't seem to know the meaning of the word. "Are they still together?"

"Not since Dad died." Gabe glanced back at the bar as if reluctant to head down the street toward it.

Morgan finally took pity on him. "We can also cut through this alley to get to my house."

"Doesn't really matter."

"Let's do it. It's actually shorter." That was a little white lie, but she found his reluctance endearing. The big, bad cowboy was afraid of ghosts.

"Yeah, well, okay, if it's shorter." He led her toward the alley.

Morgan picked her way along the dirt path between the buildings. "What happened with Jack and Josie?"

Gabe sighed. "It was probably doomed from the start. Josie loves owning a bar. There's no way she'd give it up to become a ranch wife. But Jack started slacking off on ranch work to be with her. She was free in the mornings, but that's a bad time to be gone if you're a rancher."

"Makes sense."

"Anyway, the long and short of it is that Jack was in bed with Josie when Dad called and demanded that he come home and help him fetch a horse he'd bought. Jack refused, claiming the weather was bad, which it was. Dad, stubborn to the end, went alone and...was killed in a rollover."

Morgan groaned. "And now Jack blames himself."

"Yeah."

"That explains a lot."

"Explaining it is easy. Dealing with it on a daily basis is a pain in the ass. He had no cause to be rude to you, and I plan to let him know when I get home."

Morgan hated that idea. "Don't do it, Gabe. I don't want to be the reason for more friction between you two."

"Sorry, but I'm not made that way. I invited you to be part of the parade, and the least I can expect from my family is courtesy toward you."

"But I'm a real estate agent."

"I don't care if you're a sorceress from the depths

of hell, Jack needs to respect any woman I show up with."

The image made her giggle, which meant she stopped watching where she was going and stumbled.

Gabe reacted quickly, catching her around the waist to keep her from falling. "Easy there, little lady."

As naturally as a sunflower seeks the sun, she turned in his arms and snuggled against him. "A sorceress from the depths of hell, huh?"

He cupped her bottom and brought her in tight enough to feel the solid ridge of his penis under the denim. "The sorceress part might not be so wrong. The slightest contact and I'm hard as an ax handle."

She wound her arms around his neck. "You must be a sorcerer, then, because the slightest contact and I'm juicy as a ripe watermelon."

"You would remind me about the watermelon." He tipped back the brim of his Stetson and slid his fingers through her hair until he cradled the back of her head. "Now I have to kiss you."

"What a crying shame."

"I know." He lowered his mouth until it was a breath away from hers. "I thought we could make it all the way to your house before I did this again."

"We're in a dark alley at one in the morning," she murmured. "I don't see the problem."

"Come to think of it, neither do I." His lips found hers.

No matter how many times he'd kissed her today, she still felt dizzy the moment he made contact. He stole her breath and anything resembling rational thought. The world compressed until nothing mattered but the heat generated by his supple mouth and his talented tongue.

She'd been kissed by enough men to know that Gabe was way above average with this particular skill. Either that or they were perfectly matched. Maybe it was a combination of the two.

Whatever the explanation, she couldn't confine the action to a simple kiss. As he plundered her mouth, she shoved her hands in the back pockets of his jeans. His most excellent buns flexed at the contact.

With her hands snug in his pockets, she rotated her pelvis against his and drank in his moan of lust. He responded by reaching under her T-shirt and unhooking her bra. By the time he began fondling her breasts, she was a mass of raging hormones.

He lifted his head. "This is crazy."

"Then crazy me some more, cowboy."

"I do believe I will." He moved in for another kiss and began unbuckling her belt as he backed her toward the nearest wall.

She wasn't in the mood to protest. By the time she felt the cool brick against her back, he had his hand inside her panties and was working magic with fingers as talented as the rest of him.

Abandoning her lips, he kissed his way to her ear and nibbled on the lobe, tugging gently at the small gold hoop she wore there as he plunged his fingers in deep and found her G-spot. "Is this crazy enough for you?"

She gulped in air. "Almost." She relished the press of the rough brick, the forbidden nature of sex in a semi-public place. Maybe she should be worried about her reputation, but as his thumb teased her clit, she couldn't bring herself to care about anything but this.

Then he curved his fingers and began to stroke her with a steady rhythm that melted every inhibition she possessed. She moaned with pleasure.

"Shh."

"It's…your fault."

He laughed softly. "Complaining?"

"Only if you…stop. Oh, Gabe, right there." She began to pant. "I'm coming, I'm…"

He kissed her at the critical moment, muffling her cries as he sent her careening over the brink into another tumultuous orgasm. He slid his fingers slowly back and forth, milking every last glorious contraction from her. Then he took his time easing her back to sanity.

Gently he withdrew, and as he lifted his mouth from hers, he painted her lips with a moist finger. He followed the same path with his tongue. "Almost as good as being there," he murmured. "But not quite. When we have a bed…"

Her body sang with eagerness as she imagined the pleasures that awaited her once he could fulfill his unspoken promise.

"I'm so hungry for you." He moistened her lips again with his damp fingers. "So hungry." And he kissed her, using his tongue to tell her how he'd satisfy that hunger.

She wondered if a person could possibly have too much sex in one night. She was more than willing to find out.

GABE WAS AFRAID he'd left his manners at the doorstep of Morgan's cute little bungalow. He'd paid no attention to the living room, the dining room or the kitchen. He couldn't have told anybody the color scheme or the type of furniture.

His attention was focused entirely on her bedroom, and he wasn't even particularly interested in the colors and furniture there, either. Her queen-size bed could have been a mattress on the floor for all he cared. His goal was naked and horizontal.

Fortunately Morgan seemed to have the same goal. She didn't offer him coffee or beer, didn't try to show him around the place, didn't even turn on any lights except for the one switch that activated two bedside table lamps. That worked for him.

They yanked off their boots and belts as if by mutual agreement before tumbling together onto her bed without bothering to pull down the comforter. He had her shirt and bra off before he thought of something critical.

"You'd better tell me where that box of condoms is located," he said between kisses.

"Let me get it."

He hated to end the contact sport they had going on, but obviously the condoms weren't conveniently stashed in a bedside drawer or she would have said so.

Wiggling out of his arms, she climbed off the bed and combed her hair back from her face with her fingers.

Lord almighty, if she wasn't his ultimate fantasy—a well-endowed woman wearing nothing but a pair of tight jeans. Maybe it was a good thing she'd gone to fetch those condoms. He'd had several opportunities to touch her magnificent tits, but so far he'd never seen her topless in full light. A man, especially a breast man, should take a moment to appreciate what he was being offered.

Acting on that notion, he drank in the sight of her bare and beautiful twins. Her creamy skin, dampened by his mouth and tongue, seemed to glow in the lamplight. The weight of her gifts from Mother Nature shifted invitingly as she moved, and her wine-colored nipples bobbed so sweetly.

His mouth grew moist and his penis throbbed. When she turned to leave, he moaned softly, swamped by nearly uncontrollable lust.

She turned back to him. "Is something wrong?"

"God, no. I've just never seen you topless in the light before, and you take my breath away."

She smiled. "I've never seen you bottomless in the light before, so make good use of your time while I'm gone, okay?"

He didn't have to be told twice. "You bet." While she rummaged around in her bathroom cabinet, he stripped off the rest of his clothes and tossed back the comforter and top sheet before stretching out on the smooth white sheet. He had a feeling it wouldn't stay smooth for long.

He expected her to sashay back into the room with a gleam in her eye and a smile on her rosy lips.

Instead, although she carried the promised box of condoms, she looked worried. "We need to set the alarm."

"Huh?"

She paused and her gaze swept over him, lingering with obvious interest on his stiff-as-a-board penis. The gleam he'd been hoping for earlier appeared in her eyes. "*Oh,* yeah. We definitely need an alarm."

"I hope you're not going to time me."

"Nope, but you need to be up before dawn."

"In case you hadn't noticed, I'm up now."

"Believe me, I noticed." She ran her tongue over her lips. "And I want me some of that."

Breath left his lungs in a whoosh and his voice came out sounding like a rusty hinge. "You can have whatever you want."

"Good." She set the box on the bedside table and pulled the clock radio around to face her. "But first, I'm setting the alarm."

"Morgan, we don't need that unless... Or do you have an early-morning appointment?" He should realize that a long holiday weekend might not be vacation time for a real estate agent.

"No appointments. I took time off for the Fourth."

"Then it doesn't matter when we—"

"Oh, yes, it does!" She punched a couple of buttons. "Okay, four-thirty. Done."

"Four-thirty?" Rolling to his side, he propped himself on his elbow and reached for the clock. "We're turning that off."

"No, we're not." She pulled it out of reach.

"Look, I'm not planning to sneak in and pretend I've been in my own bed all night, if that's what you're thinking. I'm a grownup and entitled to spend the night with a woman if I want to."

"That's not the point. I don't want history repeating

itself, with you not showing up at the ranch in time for your chores."

"My *chores?* I'm twenty-eight, not six!"

"Chores, like feed the chickens, gather the eggs, milk the cows—whatever it was that Jack wasn't there to do because he was in bed with Josie."

Laughing, Gabe pulled her down to the mattress. "I'm a cowboy, not a farm boy. I do manly things like ride the range. I don't gather eggs and milk cows."

"So who feeds the chickens?"

"Nobody." He straddled her hips and reached for the button on her jeans. "We don't have chickens."

"I thought for sure that you—"

"We don't have milk cows, either." He unzipped her jeans. "Lift up. This is all coming off."

She raised her hips from the mattress. "What kind of a ranch doesn't have cows and chickens?"

"I'll be happy to explain later." Dragging down her jeans and panties and tossing them to the floor beside the bed, he looked into her eyes. "When I'm not so busy." Then he allowed his gaze to travel a leisurely downward path from her lush breasts to the happy zone between her satin thighs.

"Oh." Her body quivered as the pace of her breathing increased.

He focused again on her eyes, which had darkened with anticipation. "I plan to make good on the promise I gave you back in the alley."

She swallowed. "Okay."

With a hand braced on either side of her shoulders and a knee on either side of her hips, he leaned down and kissed her, teasing her with his tongue so that she'd have no doubt what he meant. Lifting his head, he saw that her lips remained parted in complete surrender.

"We can talk about cows and chickens when I'm finished," he murmured, smiling.

Her eyes opened slowly, gradually revealing the depths of passion reflected there. Her response was a soft purr. "Or not."

"Or not." Heart racing with excitement, he began his journey. His mouth had never taken such a luxury cruise. He lingered over the smooth, perfumed skin of her breasts and the pebbled texture of each nipple before moving lower, tracing each rib.

Her skin tasted of milk and honey laced with the salty tang of the boisterous sex they'd already enjoyed. She shuddered when he dipped his tongue into her navel, as if she knew he was giving her one more preview of what lay ahead.

By the time he settled between her thighs, he was ready to explode with needs of his own. Loving her this way would be like a thirsty man drinking seawater. The more he had of her, the greater his desire.

But he craved her nectar, and he would have it, even if the pressure increased to the point of pain. Parting her silky curls, he found her rosy treasure, already dew-soaked and trembling. The first stroke of his tongue brought an urgent whimper.

"Say it," he whispered, his breath fanning the moist entrance to all her secrets.

Her answer was more plea than command. "Take me."

And take her he did, bestowing that most intimate and thorough of kisses. And as he feasted, his body grew ever hotter, ever more demanding, yet he kept on. When she began to thrash beneath him, he captured her hips in both hands and held her fast so that he could finish what he'd started.

Her cries, muted at first, grew louder until she arched off the bed and called his name. *His* name. A fierce sense of triumph gripped him, and as her tremors eased, he turned his head and nipped the tender skin of her inner thigh, not enough to hurt much, but definitely enough to leave a mark.

She gasped softly but made no protest.

Vaguely he was aware that his action was completely out of character, something he'd never considered with any other woman. But he couldn't take it back. Some instinct had propelled him to brand her.

Breathing heavily, aching from the effort to delay his own gratification, he changed his position so he could reach the condoms. He glanced over and found her watching him.

"I'm sorry." He gulped in air. "I didn't mean to—" But he couldn't finish the lie. "That's not true. I meant to."

"I know."

He fumbled with the box. "And now I need you so much my coordination's shot."

Rolling to her side, she rose up on one arm. "Just lie down, Gabe. I'll handle this."

He went still.

Her smile was pure seduction, and that promising gleam was back in her eyes.

"Okay." He handed her the box and sank back down on the mattress.

Instead of taking out a condom, she leaned over to the far side of the bed and put the box on the other nightstand. When she turned back to him, her gaze focused on his white-hot penis. "As I said before, I want some of that."

7

MORGAN THOUGHT it was only fair that she get equal time to turn Gabe inside out in the same way he'd done to her. And on top of that, he'd bitten her. Considering her determination to stay unattached until she was firmly grounded with a home and a thriving business, she shouldn't like that he'd done that.

But for some reason she didn't want to examine right now, she'd loved it. This matchup that was supposed to be a simple case of mutual lust might not be quite so simple, after all. Yet the next few minutes looked as if they could be very simple. She'd give Gabe the blow job of his life.

Judging from the way his chest heaved and his body trembled, he could use that. She didn't plan to make the process go quickly, though, no matter how tightly he was wound. Although the orgasm he'd given her had sapped her of strength, the adrenaline rush of knowing she was about to take charge of his climax had pumped energy back into her system.

Before taking her position astride his thighs, she handed him a pillow. "Prop this behind your head."

His eyebrows lifted.

"It's more fun if you watch."

"Sweetheart, it'll be a short show."

She surveyed his body, slick with sweat. She planned to make him sweat some more. "Maybe not."

"Guaranteed." His breathing grew labored. "In fact, if you don't get started soon…"

"Right." Straddling his thighs, she studied the object of her affections. He was so finely made he could probably sell a plaster cast of his penis to a sex-toy company. She could hardly wait to get her hands on him, but she had to be careful.

That's why her first move was to squeeze the base of his thick penis with her thumb and forefinger.

"Damn, Morgan, I'm going to…"

She squeezed a little harder.

He blew out a breath. "Okay, maybe not yet. But soon."

"We'll see. Don't you want to have some fun first?"

"Love to." He dragged in air. "Probably can't."

She maintained firm pressure with her thumb and first finger. "Describe one of your competitions for me."

"You're kidding."

"No, I'm not. Distract yourself for a bit. Then you can enjoy this even more."

"I've never met a woman quite like you, O'Connelli."

"Is that a compliment?"

His grin looked a bit strained. "You think I'd insult you while you have a choke-hold on my dick?"

"I suppose not."

"It was a compliment. I like you. A lot."

"I like you, too, Gabe. Now tell me how cutting-horse competition works."

"This is crazy. Just grab the box of condoms and we'll—"

"Nope." She squeezed again. "Talk to me, cow-boy."

His eyes were very blue as he held her gaze. "You have two and a half minutes."

"Oh, I think I can draw this out longer than that."

"No, during competition. That's how much time you have."

She smiled. "So you decided to play."

"Yeah, what the hell. It might work."

"So you have two and a half minutes."

"Right. In that time you and your horse cut at least one cow from the herd."

Gradually she relaxed her grip. "Sounds simple."

"It's not." His gaze stayed locked with hers.

"I suppose nothing ever is."

"Just looks that way."

"Tell me more." She ran the tip of her fingernail along the ridge on the underside of his penis.

"I have no control. It's all up to the horse."

"I thought men liked to control what was between their legs." She gripped him gently and stroked up and down, up and down.

"We do." His eyes darkened. "But in competition… we can't."

"The horse does."

"Yeah." He gulped. "By staying parallel to the cow, veering when it veers, staying hooked."

"Sounds like split-second timing." She leaned down and allowed her breasts to nudge his penis.

"It's...it's precision work." He groaned. "You're killing me."

"But you're holding on." Lazily she moved right, then left, her softness brushing against his rigidity.

"Barely, babe. Barely."

"Tell me more."

"Uh...cattle can be hard..."

"Really?" She placed a butterfly kiss on the quivering head of his dick.

"Hard to separate. We say they're......sticky."

"Mmm." Closing her fingers around his penis, she stroked upward. A drop of moisture gathered on the tip. "Sometimes sticky is good." She licked the drop away.

Gabe sucked in a breath. "I can't...hold on...much longer."

"Keep talking." Taking him into her mouth, she applied pressure while swirling her tongue over the smooth skin.

"A hot quit is...ah, Morgan, that's...nice..."

Slowly she released him. "What's a hot quit?"

He arched back against the pillow and closed his eyes. His words came in a rush. "Abandoning a cow in the middle of the action."

"Wouldn't want that." She took his penis into her mouth again and raked the underside gently with her teeth.

He groaned again. "Sure...wouldn't."

Lifting her head, she blew across the sensitive tip. "Anything more to add?" She cupped his balls and massaged gently.

"When a cow is…cut, the horse commits to working that cow." His jaw tensed. "And I hope you're committed to working…me."

"Oh, I am, cowboy. No more teasing. It's time." With firm deliberation, she took him into her mouth and began to suck. He was a big guy, but she could accommodate most of him. From the way he was moaning and panting, she thought she must be doing a decent job.

And when he finally came, his cry of release was followed by two murmured syllables uttered so softly that she almost missed hearing them. But she didn't. He'd said her name.

And that was her cue to slide down between his trembling thighs and give him one sharp nip to remember her by.

GABE HADN'T MEANT to fall asleep, but the climax Morgan had given him had totally wiped him out. He'd barely felt the nip when she bit his thigh, but it had made him smile. She was a bold woman, and he liked that. He liked that way too much. But he'd been too exhausted to question anything before he'd conked out.

Morgan must have gone to sleep right away, too, because the bedside lamps were still on when the alarm beeped at four-thirty. The second it rang, Gabe remembered that he'd meant to shut the stupid thing off before going to sleep. He hadn't, and now he'd been wrenched out of a fabulous dream in which he and Morgan walked naked along a tropical beach. He'd never been naked on a beach in his life, but he could imagine doing it with Morgan.

He wanted the dream back, so he swatted at the alarm in an attempt to turn it off.

"Don't do that." She reached over and grabbed his arm. "I need to take you back to the ranch."

He rolled over to face her. She looked all rosy and sleep-tousled, not the sort of person a guy wanted to leave when she was as naked as in his dream, and there was an untouched box of condoms sitting in full view on the bedside table.

"Come on." She planted a quick kiss in the general vicinity of his mouth and scrambled out of bed. "Get up and get dressed. I'm driving you home."

"But I don't want to leave." He sounded whiney. Clearing his throat, he lowered his voice. "Come back to bed. I'll make it worth your while."

She moved around the bedroom collecting clothes. "I'm sure you would, and don't think I'm not tempted, but we're not doing that. Jack could tell you it's not worth causing a problem in your family."

"This is one lousy morning." Gabe sat on the edge of the bed, but he had no interest in putting on the clothes Morgan tossed in his direction. "With Jack it was a recurring thing, and he refused a direct request from our dad. Nobody's called to ask me to do anything."

"Doesn't matter. Jack and your mother have to be supersensitive to the issue now. I'm already seen as a threat by both of them. I refuse to make things worse."

"You're really going to kick me out, aren't you?"

She fastened her bra over the breasts that he longed to fondle at least once more. "Yes, I am. We've had a great time, and I don't want to ruin everything by having nastiness arise because you stayed here too long."

Reluctantly Gabe began to dress. "Then at least promise to have dinner with me tonight."

"Sure." She smiled, obviously happy with his invitation. "But it's my treat in exchange for letting me ride your horse."

He looked at her and started to laugh.

"I mean… Oh, you know what I mean."

"You're welcome to ride my horse anytime." He chuckled. "You don't have to buy me dinner, either."

"But I said I would."

"But you also said you'd be forever in my debt." He waggled his eyebrows. "I'm not letting you get off with something easy like dinner. Besides, I invited you, so I'm buying."

"We'll see."

"No, I need to buy, because this dinner invitation comes with strings attached."

"Does it, now?"

He nodded. "Definite strings. I know it's not cool for a guy to ask you to dinner with an ulterior motive, so I'm telling you flat-out. There's nothing ulterior going on. I'm asking you to dinner because I want to have sex afterward. If you have a problem with that, then—"

"A problem?" She smiled. "I'd be upset if you didn't want to do that. I'd think you hadn't enjoyed yourself as much as you seemed to."

He tucked his shirt into his jeans and fastened the button. "I enjoyed it more."

"Good. But…"

He paused in the act of shoving his belt through the loops. "What?"

"I'm not looking for a permanent boyfriend."

Which was exactly what he wanted to hear. So why wasn't he overjoyed by her statement? Maybe because he was still jacked up on hormones.

His response didn't come as easily as he would have liked, but he knew what it had to be. He'd said the words often enough to other women. "I'm not looking for a permanent girlfriend, either."

"That's a relief. We're not looking for commitment. We're just…" She hesitated, seemingly unwilling to finish the sentence.

He wasn't sure how to finish it, either. There was a common term for what they were to each other, but that term was crude, and what he shared with Morgan wasn't crude.

"I guess we're fun buddies," she said.

"Okay. That works."

"Exactly. We're in it for the fun. If your mother or Jack asks, and they very well might, then tell them that."

Gabe's good humor vanished. "I don't plan on telling them a damned thing."

Her expression became endearingly earnest. "But you should, Gabe. They're worried that I'm trying to get my hooks into you, and you could put their fears to rest."

"That's part of what's bothering me. They seem to have no faith in my judgment."

"All the more reason to get you home first thing this morning. Let's go."

"Wait." He caught her wrist and pulled her back into his arms. "It goes without saying that we won't be making out in your car while it's parked in front of the ranch house."

"No, we won't." She wound her arms around his neck. "That would not be a good idea. Besides, I've outgrown car sex."

"Me, too." He combed her hair back from her face. "But I'm glad you haven't outgrown barroom sex."

"I have to say it was a first for me."

"How about that? It was a first for me, too." He lowered his head until his mouth almost touched hers. "So we lost our cherry together."

"Yeah." There was a smile in her voice.

When he kissed her, he felt something new, an emotion that he didn't usually associate with a woman he was having sex with. Maybe there was a reason he'd rejected the crude term for their relationship in favor of a more sanitized one.

Although he and Morgan had sexual chemistry to burn and he cherished that, she offered something that was even harder to find. Apparently she wanted to be his friend. With Jack acting like a dictator these days, he could use one.

MORGAN HAD NEVER driven onto Last Chance property. Although she tried to keep her attitude casual, she was awed by the place from the moment she left the main road and passed through the massive front entrance. In the pearl-gray light of early dawn, two thick lodgepole pines connected by a third horizontal pole reached into the sky, creating a daunting silhouette.

A weathered slab of wood hung from the horizontal pole. The light was dim, but Morgan knew what the sign said, so she had no trouble reading *Last Chance Ranch* flanked on either end by the interlocking *L* and *C* that formed the ranch's brand. She drove across a metal cattle guard onto a dirt road.

"And that's another thing," Gabe said. "This road should have been paved years ago, but Dad didn't want to do it. That probably means it'll never get done. I think Jack wants to turn this place into a shrine to the old man's memory."

"Roads are expensive." Morgan drove a dark green Suzuki Grand Vitara, which had served her well when showing property in the Jackson Hole area. It took the ruts in the dirt road with no problem, but she had to keep her speed down. This was one long-assed road. She pushed the buttons to lower the automatic windows. Might as well enjoy the cool morning air.

The road ran between sage-covered meadows fenced in the Wyoming tradition of buck and pole—two poles angled into the ground to create an X, with cross pieces nestled in the crotch of the X. Not a single light could be seen. In the real estate business, a long entrance road created seclusion and seemed to hint that the house at the end would be well worth the wait.

"You're right. Roads are expensive," Gabe said. "Expensive to put in and expensive to maintain. But that wasn't Dad's objection. He was never a cheap man. He just didn't want gawkers coming onto the property too easily. According to him, a dirt road discouraged people from driving in."

"So why not put a locked gate at the main road?"

"There was my dad's twisted logic. He thought that gate would make it look as if we had something so precious that we had to lock it up and people would sneak around a locked gate out of curiosity. Plus he hated the idea of stopping to get out of his truck to open it. The dirt road worked for him."

Morgan was beginning to feel as if she'd known Jonathan Chance, after all. "But not for you?"

"For one thing, it's hell pulling a loaded horse trailer down this road even in good weather. You can imagine the kind of nightmare it becomes once it starts snowing. Heavy rain's not a lot of fun, either."

Morgan had a horrible thought. "Gabe, don't tell me the rollover was on this—"

"No, it wasn't here, thank God. It happened a good twenty miles from here, on a paved road slick with rain. I was out of town, putting on a cutting-horse demonstration for some 4-H kids down in Cody." He paused. "Haven't been able to make myself do another one of those 4-H events since."

Morgan reached over and squeezed his knee. "They say the first year is the hardest."

"It wouldn't have to be quite so hard if Jack would ease up."

"Maybe he just needs time." Morgan had been furious with Jack yesterday, but now that she understood him a little better, her anger had ebbed away.

"Or a swift kick in the butt. And I might be the guy

to give it to him. Now that he's passed the big three-oh, he might be getting a little soft."

Morgan doubted it, but she had her mind on other things, like the big hip-roofed barn she'd just driven by, the outbuildings beyond that, and finally, the huge house in front of her. She'd thought of ranch houses as rambling, one-story structures. This one looked more like a two-story ski lodge, or perhaps the fantasy creation of a kid with a deluxe set of Lincoln Logs.

As the car's tires crunched to a stop on the circular gravel driveway, she glanced to her right at the center section of the house with its mammoth front door. Two wings branched out from either side and were angled in a way that reminded her of arms flung open in greeting. A front porch lined with rockers ran the length of the house, and flowers bloomed in the beds on either side of the steps.

Although the log house was immense, the effect was softened by strategic landscape lighting and the homey presence of those rocking chairs. No one would ever call this place cozy, but it was certainly welcoming. Morgan was dying to see the inside, but that wouldn't be happening this morning, and maybe not ever.

She turned to Gabe. "It's gorgeous."

"I know. It represents seventy-three years of effort."

A lump of emotion stuck in her throat. "Gabe, do you know how much I envy you that kind of heritage?"

Leaning over the console, he cradled her face in both hands. "It comes with a price," he said gently. "You envy my heritage, but I envy your freedom." He kissed her softly and released her. "I'll be at your door at six tonight."

"Sounds good."

"It sounds more than good. I'll be counting the minutes." He'd started to climb out of the SUV just as the front door opened.

Sarah Chance, dressed in jeans and a long-sleeved shirt, stepped out on the porch. "Gabe?"

"Hi, Mom."

"You'd better get down to the barn. Jack's there with Nick. There's a problem with Doozie."

"Be right there." Gabe turned back to Morgan. "Doozie's the horse I brought home and she's been a bone of contention ever since. Listen, if this turns into a thing, then I might be a little late tonight, but I'll be there."

"Don't worry about promising anything. You do what you have to in order to preserve the peace."

"I'll do whatever I have to in order to preserve my sanity, which means spending the night in your bed."

"Gabe, not so loud. Your mother might hear you."

"You know what? I kind of hope she does. I'm proud to know you, Morgan O'Connelli." With that he closed the car's passenger door and gave her a wave before striding off toward the barn.

Morgan was so intent on watching him go that she totally missed seeing Sarah Chance come around the front of the car. When she spoke, she was standing beside the open driver's window, and Morgan jumped.

"Sorry, didn't mean to scare you." Sarah cleared her throat. "But I thought I'd better grab the opportunity while you were here."

Morgan met the older woman's gaze and discovered to her shock that Gabe had Sarah's eyes. The resemblance was disconcerting, considering how much time Morgan had spent totally captured in the net of Gabe's blue eyes. During the parade, Sarah's sunglasses had hidden the resemblance.

"It's obvious that Gabe spent the night with you."

"Yes, he did." Morgan decided there was no harm in a little white lie. "But he wanted to make sure he was back here to do...whatever was necessary this morning." Morgan still wasn't clear on what that was and hoped her vagueness wouldn't hurt Gabe's cause.

"That's good to hear, but I'm not really concerned about that. We're used to having Gabe gone. He's not nearly as attached to this place as the other two. I've braced myself for the day he tells me he wants to live somewhere else."

"I can't imagine wanting to live anywhere else." Once the words were out, Morgan realized she probably shouldn't have said them, especially with the note of longing in her voice.

Sarah was quiet for a moment. "I hope for two things for my sons. One is that they find a woman they can love with all their heart. The second is that the woman returns that love with all her heart."

Morgan wanted to say that she and Gabe were all about fun, not love. But telling that to his mother wasn't quite as easy as she'd imagined.

"The point is," Sarah continued, "I'd hate for anyone to latch onto one of my boys because they fell in love with this." She gestured toward the house and barn.

Maybe honesty was the best policy. "I'm already in

love with what you have here. But I'm not an opportunist, and even if I were, Gabe's too smart to fall for
somebody who's only using him."

Sarah's eyebrows lifted in a gesture so reminiscent
of Gabe that Morgan caught her breath.

"Let me put your mind at ease, Mrs. Chance. I'm a
little jealous of the fact that your family has been here
for three generations, but I am not in love with your
son and he's not in love with me. We're enjoying being
together, but we're not serious about each other."

"If you can say that, then you don't fully understand
Gabe, and that worries me."

"I beg your pardon?"

"When my son thinks enough of a woman to loan
her his horse, it's very serious."

8

GABE RUBBED a hand over his day-old beard as he headed for the barn. He probably looked like some cowpoke down on his luck, when in fact he'd never felt better in his life. Great sex could do that for a guy.

But he needed to forget about Morgan for now and concentrate on Doozie, the bay mare he'd saved from the auction block a few weeks ago. Her owner, Brad Bennington, had given up on her, convinced that her injuries, which caused her to founder, would cost him more money and time than he wanted to invest.

Gabe knew what would have happened on the auction block. A horse with Doozie's condition would end up at the slaughterhouse, and he wasn't going to let that happen. True, founder was the same thing that had precipitated the death of the great racehorse Barbaro, but Gabe didn't believe Doozie would die. So he'd brought her home to the Last Chance, because the ranch was dedicated to last chances.

The lights were on in the barn as he approached. Butch and Sundance, two dogs Nick had found wandering along the highway, had taken up sentry duty on each side of the barn door. Butch was a mixed breed, mostly boxer, and Sundance looked like a border collie, although chances were he wasn't a purebred, either. Gabe paused briefly to give them each a scratch. If Nick could rescue dogs, then Gabe figured he could rescue a horse.

But Jack hadn't been pleased when Gabe had brought Doozie home. She was hurt, and she wasn't a paint, so Jack wouldn't want to breed her. Gabe had known all that, but when faced with the knowledge that the young mare was destined to become dog food, he hadn't been able to turn away. Doozie had a whole life in front of her, providing his brother Nick could cure her. And Nick was a top-notch vet.

Inside the barn he breathed in the sweet mix of hay and horses. Seeing the place as Morgan might, he had a new appreciation for the old barn, which had been on the property when his Grandpa Archie brought his bride to the ranch. The barn had been through several renovations since then, but much of the original structure remained.

Gabe found himself thinking of how much Morgan would enjoy walking around in here, listening to stories of his grandparents' adventures starting married life in a barn. He wanted to share that with her, but bringing her here would only make her uncomfortable. Jack might naturally assume Morgan was casing the joint so she could find a way to make a profit from her association with one of the Chance boys. As for his mother, she'd always said that she wanted him to find a woman who loved him beyond all reason, and that wasn't Morgan.

Jack leaned over the open door of Doozie's stall talking to someone, probably Nick, who was no doubt crouched down working on the mare's hoof. Doozie herself stood patiently, her coat gleaming in the light from the overhead bulb.

Gabe walked down the aisle between the stalls, pausing to stroke the muzzles of the horses poking their heads out to see who was there. Calamity Jane, the paint mare who had foaled last month and who was his favorite horse in the barn, clearly expected a treat. Gabe would have to bring her one later.

Jack glanced up. "Here comes lover boy looking like he just rolled out of bed. Have a good time?"

"That's none of your damned business."

His brother nodded. "I'll take that as an affirmative. A talkative guy is usually making up stuff. A silent man got what he went after."

Gabe's jaw tightened. "I don't think you and I should talk about Morgan, not after the way you treated her."

Jack's dark eyes gave nothing away. "You're probably right about that." He tugged on the brim of his black Stetson and gestured toward the stall. "Your horse is not improving on schedule, little brother. That means she may or may not recover, and in the meantime, she's costing the ranch a bundle."

"Since when are you all about the bottom line, Jack?"

"Since Dad's will put me in charge of it. I intend to keep this place solvent, and I can't do it if we start leaking money for no good reason."

Gabe decided not to waste his breath arguing the

point. There was a time when Jack would have thought saving a good horse was reason enough, even if that horse never made a dime for the Last Chance. His heart used to contain a large soft spot for animals in trouble.

The new Jack had become a Grinch, and Gabe was still trying to decide what to do about that. In the meantime, he needed to see about his horse. He walked into the stall.

Nick was in the midst of refitting the special shoe that allowed Doozie to stand on her injured leg without quite so much pain. "I'm doing what I can." His gaze flicked up to meet Gabe's. "But she's not responding the way I'd hoped."

"I'm sorry to hear that." Gabe held the mare's halter and stroked the perfect white blaze that ran from her forelock to her nose, like a racing stripe. "Hey, girl. You gotta fight, okay? Nick can only do so much, but part of this process is you wanting to get better."

Jack blew out a breath. "Jesus. Are we into woo-woo healing, now?"

"Why not, if it works," Nick said as he finished adjusting the shoe and stood. "She has an air of resignation about her, as if she's given up. I hate to say this, but she doesn't seem happy here."

Jack threw up his hands. "Obviously we need to improve her accommodations, then! Let's turn the barn into a horsey day spa. Hey, we can pipe in music and maybe hire a shrink to analyze her inner feelings."

Gabe glanced at him. "Bite me, Jack."

"Oh, grow up, Gabe."

"Hey, you're the one who's regressing into some kind of anal prick!"

Jack rolled his eyes. "Regressing, am I? Okay, maybe we need to import several shrinks, one for the horse, and one for each of us, so we can all get in touch with our feelings."

Nick packed up his supplies. "Might not be a bad idea."

"God, don't you start, too!" Jack glared at both of them. "Look, you gave her a chance, Gabe. You brought her to the best vet in Wyoming, probably the best vet in the western states. If she can't recover here, she's not meant to recover. We should all cut our losses and—"

"She needs a goat." Gabe mentally slapped himself on the forehead. "Why didn't I think of that before? She's used to having one in her stall! I should've bought the goat when I bought her, and I didn't even think of it. Let me make some phone calls and see if it's still available."

Jack stared at him as if he'd lost his mind. "*Hel*-lo. Is this goat going to be free?"

"Of course not. I'll have to buy it from Bennington, assuming he kept it."

"If you get as good a deal on the goat as you did on the horse, I might as well file for bankruptcy now and save a little time."

"Dammit, Jack, it's just a goat!"

"And I'm not going to approve the purchase of said goat! We're already into this horse for more money than I care to think about."

Gabe took off his Stetson and ran his fingers along

the brim as he fought to keep his temper. "So you're not going to approve the purchase of the goat," he said quietly.

Nick picked up his medical kit and stood. "Never mind. I'll buy the goat."

"No, you won't," Gabe said. "I appreciate the peace-keeping move on your part, but I'll buy the goat. I'll be getting entry-fee refunds that should cover it." But even as he said that, he was aware it was all ranch money. At this point, Jack was in total control of their finances.

When their dad had been alive, each son had drawn a salary for work done around the ranch. Jack had always made more because he handled more responsibility, or he had until hooking up with Josie last summer.

Gabe hadn't been home to hear the fights between his dad and Jack, but Nick had reported they were loud and angry, with their dad threatening to cut Jack's pay and Jack threatening to leave the ranch. The issue had remained unresolved and simmering as summer became fall. And then Jonathan Chance was killed.

Once Nick had his veterinary license, he'd had a way to earn money other than ranch work. He had a few other clients in the area, so if the ranch disappeared tomorrow, he would be okay financially.

As for Gabe, he'd never thought much about money. He'd had enough for his simple needs, and the Last Chance had paid for his competition every summer and the upkeep on his horses. He'd donated any prize money back to the ranch. The system had suited him fine. Until now.

Maybe Jack was right. Maybe he needed to grow up. For ten years he'd concentrated all his energy on training cutting horses and winning competitions. Without the support of the Last Chance, he couldn't have done that and couldn't continue to do it. Maybe he needed to get a fix on where his life was going and exactly who was in the saddle making the decisions.

But he also realized something else. He'd listened to the reading of the will, and it had clearly specified that the ranch belonged to all of them, not just Jack. If a dispute arose, each of them, including his mom, had an interest in the ranch.

If anyone wanted to sell, the other three had to buy out the fourth person, which would undoubtedly require taking out a loan or selling off some acreage. Gabe figured his dad hadn't expected this to happen, but he'd put the contingency in the will so that nobody would be forced to stay here. Gabe wanted to stay, at least part of the time, but Jack was making that option less and less palatable.

"Oh, for Christ's sake." Jack blew out a breath. "Get the effing goat. But that better work."

"Or what, Jack?" Gabe walked out of the stall and faced his older brother. "Let's put all our cards on the table. I brought Doozie here to give her sanctuary. You seem to be putting a dollar limit on how much sanctuary she deserves."

"Somebody has to!"

"Do they?" Gabe held Jack's gaze. "Is the Last Chance in such bad financial shape?"

"Not at the moment, but that doesn't mean we can afford to throw money away. Besides keeping us housed and fed, this ranch provides a living for a bunch of cowboys, plus Mary Lou. I have a responsibility to keep us in the black so we can continue the way we have in the past."

"Nice speech." Gabe put on his hat and tugged the brim down. "But if I remember my history right, Archie and Nelsie dedicated this place to giving both people and animals a last chance at happiness. You can't put a dollar value on that." He turned to leave, but swung back as he thought of something else.

"About Morgan," he said.

Nick groaned. "I don't think now's the time to discuss—"

"No, let him say his piece." Jack crossed his arms over his chest. "What about this real estate agent, Gabe?"

"I've decided to invite her out here this afternoon. If she can make it, we'll saddle a couple of horses and go for a ride around the ranch."

His brother's eyes narrowed. "Why?"

"Because she's a friend of mine and she'd love seeing it."

Jack's derisive snort said it all.

"So help me, Jack, if you do anything to make her feel uncomfortable while she's here, I'll clean your clock."

"You can try."

"Don't give me a reason." Gabe almost wished Jack would provoke him into a fight. Years ago Gabe hadn't been able to hold his own against Jack, but he sure as hell could now, and he was itching to prove it.

AT THREE that afternoon, against her better judgment, Morgan drove back down the long dirt road to the ranch house. Gabe had promised her a tour of the house before they took their horseback ride. Eagerness to see the inside of the house and the surrounding acreage vied with her dread of running into either Jack or Sarah.

Gabe had promised to make sure she wasn't treated like a smear of dung on the bottom of somebody's boot. Morgan wasn't convinced, but she couldn't resist getting a peek inside the house and then spending the rest of the afternoon riding the range with cowboy Gabe. As she'd observed during the parade, he looked mighty fine astride a horse.

He was sitting in one of the porch rockers when she pulled up, his hat tilted back, his booted feet out in front of him, and a grin on his face that made her heart lurch with joy. She was alarmingly glad to see him. On a gladness scale of one to ten, she'd rate this moment a fifty.

Unfolding himself from the rocker, he picked up a straw Western hat from the chair beside him and ambled down the porch steps. She'd be willing to bet he'd brought that hat for her to keep her from getting burned during the ride. The thoughtful gesture touched her.

As she climbed out of her SUV, she fought the urge to run around it and fling herself into his arms. They were, after all, right in front of the house with its many windows. If Morgan were Gabe's mother, she'd station herself at one of them to observe the interloper's arrival.

A disapproving mother was a new experience for Morgan. She made friends easily, and mothers of the guys she'd dated had always liked her. She still kept in touch with a couple of them, even though their sons had married other women.

But in those cases, the mothers had been pleased that Morgan wasn't ready to get married right away. They'd wanted their sons to finish their degrees or achieve career goals before settling down. Apparently Sarah held the opposite view. She thought Gabe was serious about Morgan, which meant Morgan should be serious about Gabe.

Yet that wasn't how Morgan understood the situation at all. Gabe had flat-out said he wasn't looking to make a commitment. Maybe he needed to tell his mother that. Morgan felt misjudged, and that wasn't the least bit pleasant.

Because of Gabe's mother, she had dressed conservatively, playing down her considerable assets by choosing a vertically-striped blouse that she left hanging out instead of tucked into her jeans.

Gabe met her before she made it to the rear bumper. Setting both her hat and his on the top of the SUV, he blocked her way. "I just need one kiss."

"Gabe, we shouldn't—" That was as much of a protest as she managed before he swept her into his arms and covered her mouth with his.

Instead of pushing him away as she'd planned, she curled her fingers into the soft cotton of his freshly laundered shirt. Obviously he'd shaved and showered not long ago. He smelled great and tasted even better. When she cupped the back of his head, his hair was still damp.

"Mmm." He coaxed her lips apart and gave her a very sexy thrust of his tongue.

By the time he finally let her go, she staggered a little, no longer steady on her feet.

He caught her by the shoulders. "Okay?"

She looked into his laughing blue eyes and couldn't help smiling back at him. "You're a devil. I drive in here all cool and collected, ready to take a sedate tour of the house and surrounding grounds, and you—"

"Who said it would be sedate?"

"*Gabe.* I'm trying to make a good impression here."

He surveyed her. "And you look terrific. The turquoise stripes in that blouse match your eyes. Great choice. Personally, I'd prefer to see that blouse tucked in, but that's just me."

"Precisely why I didn't tuck it in. I'm not here to please you."

"We'll see about that." He gave her a slow smile.

"What do you mean?"

"Never mind. Here's your hat. Let's go check out the house." He took his Stetson by the brim and settled it on his head.

She caught his arm before he rounded the back of the SUV. "Gabe Chance, what are you up to?"

He gave her an innocent look. "Who, me?"

"Listen, we are not going to make out in that house. I don't care how big it is or how sturdy the locks are on the doors. It's still your mother's house, and besides, it's the middle of the day."

"Okay, we won't make out in the house. How about in the barn? Could we do it there?"

"No! If this is what you have in mind, I'll get right back in the SUV. I know that at least two of your family members are worried about me being here, and I'm not going to make it worse by having sex with you right under their noses."

He nodded, looking like a contrite little boy. He all but kicked the dirt with his toe. "You're absolutely right. I don't know what I was thinking."

She didn't trust that mock-serious tone of his for a minute. She didn't trust herself all that much, either. Once he got hold of her, she turned to putty in his hands.

She needed to set the ground rules before they proceeded on this tour. "Here's the deal, Gabe. I want you to promise me that you don't have seduction on your mind."

He gazed down at her, his lips twitching as if he wanted to laugh. "Morgan, whenever I lay eyes on you, I have seduction on my mind. That's the way it is."

"Then I'll just go back to town and we'll forget all about this tour."

"Hey." He massaged her upper arms. "I was teasing you a minute ago. I wouldn't take a chance on embarrassing you by trying to have sex in the house or in the barn."

"Good. I'm glad to know you have some sense after all."

His grin finally broke through. "Yeah, the house and the barn would be a stupid place to have sex. But out in the woods…now, that's a whole other situation."

9

INITIALLY GABE had had pure intentions for this invitation. He'd meant to show Morgan around and wait until tonight, after their dinner at Spirits and Spurs, to get down with the luscious Morgan O'Connelli. But after she'd agreed to drive out here, he'd started thinking about taking that long horseback ride, and how nice and remote parts of the ranch could be. Possibilities began to form in his hormone-soaked brain.

Still, he wouldn't rush her through the tour of the house and the barn. He hadn't asked her why she'd ended up in real estate, but it didn't take a genius to figure it out. Her family had never owned a home, and Morgan obviously had longed for one. By going into real estate, she could immerse herself in the joy of finding homes for others.

Whatever else the Last Chance represented, it was most certainly a home. As he ushered Morgan through the front door and she gave a little sigh of delight, he paused and took another look, trying to see the living area as she was seeing it.

After all these years, he took the comfortable setting

for granted, but she wouldn't. She might picture herself tucked into one of the overstuffed armchairs grouped in front of the massive stone fireplace. Or maybe she'd imagine the two of them on the love seat sipping cocoa as the flames crackled. He liked that idea.

"What a spectacular room." She glanced up at the wagon-wheel chandelier with antique oil lamps that had been wired for electricity. "That's very cool."

"My grandfather made it." Gabe felt an unexpected rush of pride and discovered he was eager to give her details. "He and his brother-in-law Seth built this center section pretty much by themselves with a little help from my grandmother."

"The fireplace, too?"

"Yep. My grandfather's trade was carpentry, with some training in masonry, but then the Depression hit and he was out of work. He won the ranch in a card game and decided to move out here. At least he'd have a roof over his head and food from the garden."

"I admire that kind of pluck." She put her hand on the banister of the curved staircase leading to the second floor. "This is elegant."

"I know. I'm convinced that both Archie and Nelsie had artistic talent. My dad could sketch, but he never thought he had time. He'd planned to do some drawing in his retirement. Nick's like him in that way. Not me, though."

"You're creative in other ways." Her easy smile explained exactly what she was talking about.

Ah, she had no idea. Their saddlebags were already packed with everything they'd need to get creative out in the woods.

"What's in there?" She gestured through a door on the right side of the room.

"My dad's office. Jack's office now, although I still think of it as belonging to my dad."

"Your dad will always be a part of this place, just like your grandfather and grandmother and your mom. That's awesome, Gabe."

"Yeah, I guess it is." He was glad he'd brought her here. She was putting things into perspective for him, reminding him of what was at stake.

She began strolling the perimeter of the room and stared up at the large Native American rugs on the wall. There were three, and each was at least eight by ten, although Gabe had never measured them.

"These look like authentic Navajo," she said.

"Straight from the reservation in Arizona. After Seth moved to Phoenix with his wife, Joyce, my grandparents made a trip to see them and came back with several pots of cactus and three big rugs. The cactus died, but the rugs have been hanging there ever since."

"And now they're worth a fortune." Gabe's mother came in from the hallway that ran the length of the left wing, where the kitchen and dining room were located, along with Mary Lou's private set of rooms.

As the only two women on the ranch, Sarah and Mary Lou had developed a deep friendship. Usually if Gabe wanted to find his mother, his first stop was the kitchen. If his mom wasn't there, Mary Lou could tell him where to find her.

"But you may already know that," his mother added, walking over toward Morgan. "Welcome to our home."

Gabe held his breath and hoped for the best. That statement about the rugs could be taken as a flung gauntlet, as if his mother thought Morgan was sizing up the treasures in the house. Or it could be nothing more than an idle comment.

He'd promised Morgan that no one would cause her distress while she was here, but it had been an empty promise, he realized now. A guy couldn't control how his family behaved.

Morgan smiled pleasantly. "Thank you. And as a matter of fact, I do know these rugs are valuable. I moved around a lot as a kid. We spent a few months camped near a trading post. I was fascinated by the looms. Still am."

"Me, too." Gabe's mother fingered the edge of a cream, red and black-patterned rug. "I like to think I could learn to do that, but I don't know that I'd have the patience."

Gabe relaxed a little. His mother was making conversation. That was a good sign. Maybe she'd realized her first reaction to Morgan had been more of the knee-jerk variety.

"I know I wouldn't be able to do it." Morgan moved her finger over an intricate part of the design. "Just look at that. Threading a loom to achieve that pattern would require a gift for math besides infinite patience." She glanced at Gabe's mother. "It's mind-boggling what those women could accomplish. It puts my little cross-stitched pillows in the shade."

Sarah met her gaze. "You do cross-stitch?"

"When I have the time, which isn't often lately. It's a soothing hobby."

"I know what you mean. I should get back to it."

Gabe knew his mother well enough to realize she was warming toward Morgan. He relaxed a little more.

"By the way," Sarah continued. "Have you seen Gabe's trophies yet?" She gestured toward a display case in the corner.

"Not yet."

"That boy does us proud. Come on over here and take a look."

Gabe's jaw dropped. His mother wasn't just making conversation, she was making overtures! Well, that was good, wasn't it? Confused but happy, he followed the women over to the display case.

His mother could have simply pointed out what was in there, but no, she opened the double doors and picked up the trophies one by one so Morgan could hold them. In each case his mother explained when he'd won the award and how special it was. Gabe began to squirm. It almost seemed as if his mom had decided to do a sales job to convince Morgan he was the catch of the year.

Then the light dawned. Shoshone was a small town, and his mother was well-connected. She'd probably spent the morning on the phone finding out everything there was to know about Morgan O'Connelli.

The reports must have been good, so Sarah had decided to reconsider her stance. She and Morgan had discovered common ground in their mutual admiration of the Navajo rugs and in cross-stitching. And now... damned if his mom wasn't acting as if she had her eye on a prospective daughter-in-law.

Good Lord. But he could understand the impulse. His mother's world had been knocked off kilter last fall, and he could see why she'd find comfort in having each of her sons settled with families of their own. Then she could look toward the future and the prospect of a fourth generation growing up on the Last Chance.

Fortunately Nick and Dominique were in line to make that dream come true. Gabe wasn't ready and neither was Morgan. But he dreaded the moment when he had to disillusion his mother and tell her that he and Morgan weren't headed in that direction.

This new disaster-in-the-making was mostly his fault. He'd brought Morgan out here, which his mother was incorrectly interpreting as a sign that he had serious feelings for her. The reality was, he'd brought her here to show Jack and his mother that they weren't controlling his actions. Damn, this was getting complicated.

Finally Sarah exhausted the contents of the trophy case. "Has Gabe shown you the kitchen and dining room?" she asked.

"She just got here a little bit ago, Mom," he said. "Right before you walked in. I haven't had a chance to take her around."

"Then come with me, Morgan. You, too, Gabe, if you want, although you've seen all this a thousand times so you can relax in here until we come back."

"No, I'll come with you." He wasn't about to let his mother hijack this tour any more than she already had. Next she was liable to get out his baby pictures.

"Mary Lou!" his mother called as they headed down the hall. "Put the coffee on! I'm bringing you a visitor!"

Gabe stifled a groan. He would have been happy

with a polite welcome followed by a discreet disappearing act. Instead his mom was rolling out the red carpet and turning this into a coffee klatch. He thought about Top Drawer and Finicky, saddled and waiting outside the barn. He thought of the condom he'd stashed in the saddlebags. At this rate, he'd never get to use it.

MORGAN SMILED to herself as she walked with Sarah down the hall, Gabe trailing behind. The poor guy couldn't catch a break. First his mother had been distant and he'd been embarrassed about that. Now she'd swung in the opposite direction and seemed determined to welcome Morgan into the family. Gabe's expression had been priceless. He was so not into this new program.

The poor woman apparently thought her son had wedding bells on his mind when all he wanted was sex and a few laughs. That was all Morgan wanted, too. Sure, she was captivated by this ranch house and its history, but she wasn't ready to be anyone's wife or raise anyone's grandchildren. This house cried out for grandchildren to carry on the Chance legacy.

The hallway was bordered by windows on the left, which looked out on the porch and a spectacular view of the Tetons. To the right was a rogues' gallery of family pictures interspersed with doors that Sarah explained were a series of storage closets.

Morgan slowed, wanting to look at the pictures lining the wall. One was of a very little boy on a very large horse. She could swear that towhead was—

"That's Gabe on his first horse," Sarah said.

"Jonathan didn't believe in starting them on ponies, so the boys rode full-size horses from the time they were three."

"Impressive." Morgan glanced back at Gabe, who rolled his eyes.

"Look at this one," Sarah said. "It's of all three boys, and Gabe wasn't even a year old yet. He was such an adorable little—"

Gabe made a gagging sound.

Sarah spun in his direction. "Gabriel Archibald Chance, stop that. Honestly."

"Mom, I'm sure Morgan isn't interested in my baby pictures."

"Sure I am." The minute Morgan admitted her curiosity, she realized she'd made a tactical mistake. Wanting to see a guy's baby pictures was the mark of a woman who dreamed of the babies they could make together.

And that wasn't her. She simply wanted to see the pictures because...well, because he'd been a really cute kid. Everybody liked to admire cute kids.

"See?" Sarah gestured toward Morgan. "She's not bored in the least."

Gabe sighed. "She's just being polite."

Sarah waggled a finger at him. "And you're being a pain for some reason. Okay, I'll leave you two to finish up the pictures and I'll go find out if Mary Lou has brownies to go with the coffee. That should make you happy, Gabe."

"Thanks, Mom."

As Gabe's mother started back down the hall, Gabe caught Morgan's hand and lowered his voice so only she could hear him. "Sorry about this. Somehow she's gotten the wrong idea."

Morgan squeezed his hand. "No problem."

"I just didn't want you to think I told her anything that would make her think we were a couple."

"It's not what you told her. It's what you did."

He looked puzzled. "I don't know what you mean."

"You let me ride your horse. In her mind, that's like giving me an engagement ring."

"Now that's ridiculous."

"Of course it is, but she made a big deal out of it when she talked to me this morning."

"She talked to you?"

Morgan hadn't meant to discuss that conversation with Gabe but she couldn't keep it to herself now. "After you left for the barn, she came around the car to have a word with me. Several words, in fact."

"About what?"

"She wants you to find a woman who sincerely loves you and isn't just swept away by the beauty of this ranch."

"That was nervy of her." His expression was unreadable. "And what did you say to that?"

"I told her the truth, that we weren't in love with each other."

An emotion flickered in his blue eyes and then was gone. "I'll bet you didn't say the relationship was all about sex."

"No, I'm not that brave. But she wouldn't have believed me, anyway. She said that when you thought enough of a woman to loan her your horse, then the relationship was serious."

"Oh, boy." Gabe massaged the back of his neck. "I had no idea she was reading that kind of significance into it."

"I didn't know what to say because I don't know your history of women and horses. Maybe if you point out to her that you've loaned your horse several times before, and it didn't lead to a proposal, she'll back off."

"Well, I could do that, except…"

"Except what?"

"You're the first woman I've ever let ride one of my horses."

"Oh." That thrilled her, which probably wasn't good. She shouldn't love knowing that she was in an exclusive category when it came to the women Gabe knew.

"Even worse, I was planning to put you up on Top Drawer again when we go on our trail ride around the ranch. If my mother happened to look out the window toward the barn, she would have seen both horses saddled and ready to go."

"Guess you should have saddled up some old nag for me to ride."

He laughed. "We're fresh out of those. Last Chance horseflesh is primo, at least according to the literature we put out. My dad wouldn't have it any other way, and Jack's continuing the tradition. I guess that's why he has such a problem with the horse I brought home. She may never be primo."

"Doozie, right?"

"Right. I have a call in to Bennington, the guy I bought her from, to see if I can get his goat."

Morgan blinked. "You want to make him mad?"

"No, I literally need his goat, the one who was Doozie's buddy. I think she's grieving for that goat. Horses and goats sometimes hang out together, and I should have realized Doozie needed her friend. That might turn things around for that horse and give her the will to pull through."

"That's cool, Gabe." Morgan smiled at him. "I like this connection you have with animals. It's something else I missed growing up. We couldn't have pets, because we moved so much and never knew if they'd be allowed in the next rental unit we found."

"If we can ever get this tour into high gear, I'll take you down to the barn so you can meet Doozie, plus the ranch dogs, and maybe some of the other horses. I wasn't planning on spending all this time in the house."

"How long have the horses been saddled?"

"I saddled them right before you got here, so not too long, and they don't mind standing there. It's shady."

Morgan glanced at her watch. "But are we going to have time to take that ride?"

"The ride can be as short or as long as we want it to be. Mostly we need to make sure we get to a certain little spot by the creek."

"Why? Is there something special you want to show me there?"

His smile was sinfully sexy. "Yes, ma'am, there sure

is. And in order to fully appreciate it, you need to be naked."

Heat sizzled through her and settled between her thighs. "Let's see if we can get the coffee and brownies to go."

_10_

GABE FELT a little guilty asking for coffee in a thermos and brownies in a bag, but not too guilty. He didn't need Mary Lou also bonding with Morgan, and both women looked as if they could do that in no time.

"Where are you two headed?" Mary Lou's sly question was the sort she would have asked when Gabe was seventeen and taking a girl out for a moonlit ride.

Unlike when he was seventeen, Gabe didn't blush when he answered. "Probably into the meadow a ways. The wildflowers are pretty out there and the view's nice. After that we'll see how much time we have."

Mary Lou nodded. Gabe was sure she knew exactly what he had in mind. Although she'd settled into plump middle age and no longer cared about styling her gray, flyaway hair, Gabe had a vivid picture of Mary Lou down by the creek in a red bathing suit years ago.

Even though he'd been a kid, maybe eight or so, he'd recognized that Mary Lou looked good in that red suit. No doubt she'd had her share of lovers, but she'd never married. She'd claimed that because she wasn't able to have kids and always intended to support herself, she couldn't see the point in a legal contract.

His mother sipped her coffee. "Are you putting Morgan on Top Drawer or Finicky?"

Another loaded question. He knew now that his mother thought the whole horse thing was a signal that he would soon drop to one knee and propose to the bodacious Miss O'Connelli. "Morgan's used to Top Drawer, so I thought she should stick with the horse she already knows."

Smiling benevolently, Sarah gestured to the hat Morgan held in one hand. "I see you're loaning her one of Roni's hats."

"Yeah, one of her old ones. I didn't think she'd mind if I borrowed it."

Morgan turned to him. "Roni? Do you have a sister I don't know about?"

"Not exactly. She showed up as a runaway teen a few years ago."

His mother put down her mug. "My husband was such a softy. That girl hot-wired one of our trucks and was going to make off with it. Jonathan caught her, and instead of turning her over to the sheriff, he promised her room and board if she'd keep our vehicles running."

Mary Lou poured herself more coffee. "Roni's good people. I miss her now that she's gone off to work on the NASCAR circuit. I was hoping she'd stick around."

"Nah, she's all about pistons and gears, not saddles and reins." Gabe thought about Roni's determination to be a NASCAR mechanic, no matter what she had to do to make that happen. He loved cutting-horse competition, but he wondered if he loved it the way Roni loved racing.

Morgan held up the hat. "I'm glad she left this behind. I appreciate the loan."

"And we have to get going." Gabe figured the barn tour was getting shorter by the minute. He needed at least an hour for his other plans, and the clock was ticking its way toward dinner.

"You got anything for the mosquitoes?" Mary Lou asked.

"No." Gabe realized that might be an oversight.

"I can't imagine we'll need mosquito repellent in broad daylight," Morgan said.

"Depends." Mary Lou reached into a cupboard and pulled out a metal spray can. "This is environmentally friendly stuff and doesn't stink too bad. I've never given it a true test, but it'll be better than nothing. If you spend any time down by the creek, you'll need it." She handed the can to Morgan, but she turned and winked at Gabe.

Oh, yeah. Mary Lou knew exactly what was going on. Gabe's special makeout spot was down by the creek. Each of the boys had staked out their own area for getting it on with a girl. Nick's was in a little forest clearing and Gabe's was a sandy spot next to the creek. Jack had a place, too, but he'd never revealed where it was except to say that his brothers would never find it.

"Are you going to show her the Shoshone sacred site?" his mother asked.

"Maybe not this trip." Gabe didn't want to load the excursion with any more significance than it already had.

Morgan glanced up at him. "What's that?"

"I'll tell you on the way. Let's go." He flashed his mother and Mary Lou a smile. "Thanks for the coffee and brownies."

"Nice meeting you, Mary Lou," Morgan said over her shoulder as Gabe grabbed her hand and hustled her out of the kitchen. "Thanks for the tour, Mrs. Chance!"

"Call me Sarah!" his mother shouted back from the kitchen. "Oh, wait a minute!" She appeared in the doorway. "This is Dominique's last night before she flies back to Indiana, so we're having a nice dinner for her here. Gabe, you should bring Morgan."

He was caught. "Well, the thing is, I—"

"I'm sure you can manage it, Gabe," his mother said. "Pam will be here." She turned to Morgan. "Have you met Pam Mulholland?"

"Not yet. But I know she owns the Bunk and Grub B and B right outside of town."

"That's Pam, and she's around here all the time. She's like family. Well, technically, she *is* family, but that's a long story."

"And we should get going," Gabe said.

"I know, I know. What's that western cliché? You're burning daylight. But Morgan, you should meet Pam. A number of her guests have ended up moving here. You could leave some of your cards with her."

"That would be wonderful," Morgan said.

"So you two will be here for dinner, then?"

Gabe knew when he was beat. "Sure, Mom. We'll be here. See you!" He steered Morgan through the large dining room with its four round wooden tables that could seat thirty-two if necessary. The family dinner tonight would be in the more intimate dining room adjacent to this one.

"Have fun!" his mother called after them.

Finally they reached the hallway. "My God, what have I done?" Gabe kept up a brisk pace on the off chance his mother would come up with some other critical message she had to deliver immediately. "You're her new best friend."

"Apparently I've passed muster, so she wants to convince me that you're a great catch."

"And here I thought I might have to protect you from her."

"You still do, in a way. You'll have to gently tell her that I'm not ready to settle down and breast-feed your children, aka her grandchildren."

Gabe screeched to a halt and stared at her. "What did you say?"

"I could be wrong, but unconsciously she might see me as nourishing a whole brood of babies."

"That's crazy." But now that she'd mentioned it, the mental image of her cradling a baby who nursed happily at her breast was stuck in his brain.

He had no intention of getting married right now, let alone fathering children, but if he'd planned to do either, he'd want a woman like Morgan. Morgan would do nicely. Except he wasn't in the market.

"You know what we need?" He wrenched open the front door. "We need fresh air. We can tour the barn when we get back."

"Whatever you say. You're the tour guide."

"Damn straight. And I say let's ride."

She held out the spray can of mosquito repellent. "Want to tuck this in your saddle bag?"

"Yeah." He took it from her as they crossed the yard to the saddled horses. "It might come in handy."

"If the creek attracts mosquitoes, we could avoid that area."

"No, we couldn't. You'll like it there."

"Is that where you're going to show me something special?"

He glanced into her laughing eyes. "Exactly."

MORGAN FELT as if she'd stepped into a Wyoming publicity shoot—snow-tipped mountains, flower-strewn meadow and a cowboy and cowgirl riding high-stepping paints through the landscape. She was becoming attached to Gabe's roan paint and had the vain thought that Top Drawer probably looked good with her hair, too.

Next to her, Gabe made a striking picture mounted on his other cutting horse. Finicky was a chocolate-and-white paint who picked his way carefully around mud puddles. Thus his name, according to Gabe.

Morgan tried not to spend too much time noticing the way Gabe's tight buns fit into that leather saddle. Sitting astride her own saddle with its gentle rocking motion naturally made her think of sex, especially when she focused on the fit of Gabe's jeans.

Conversation might be the answer to her problem, and Sarah had brought up a couple of topics Morgan was curious about. "So what's this sacred site I'm not going to see today?"

"It's a flat granite rock with veins of white quartz running through it."

"That's it? Just a rock?"

"A big rock. You could dance the two-step on it."

"Have you?" Morgan had been treated to Gabe's two-stepping skills during the street dance.

"No, but it would be fun. We'll have to try it sometime. I think the Shoshones used to dance on it back in the day, but I don't think many members of the tribe go out there anymore."

"But they could? They're allowed access?"

"Absolutely. Once Grandpa Archie figured out that the ranch included an area the Shoshones considered sacred, he encouraged them to visit whenever they felt like it. For a while they did, but not so much these days."

Now Morgan really wanted to see this rock. "How close are we?"

"We're headed in the opposite direction."

"Oh."

"Hey, it's just a rock. Nick will tell you it has mystical powers, but I think that's BS."

Morgan smiled to herself. Gabe was the same guy who'd freaked out when she'd reported seeing a ghost. Apparently the idea of paranormal events scared the pants off him.

She wouldn't push it. But the lazy gait of her horse was still working on her, and she couldn't hear the sound of a creek yet, so they weren't close to the place where Gabe would show her *something special*.

She was more than ready for that something special, but they couldn't very well get it on in the middle of an open meadow. So they could talk. "Your mom mentioned something about Pam connected with a long story. What's that about?"

"You don't really want to hear all this family history, do you?"

"How close are we to the creek?"

"Another fifteen or twenty minutes."

"Then tell me a story. Otherwise I'm liable to jump your bones right here."

He laughed and allowed his gaze to take a leisurely trip over her warm and achy body. "Good to know."

"Stop teasing me. Talk."

He smiled. "I hate to douse the flames. The more worked up you are, the better—"

"Talk, damn it!"

"Okay, okay. I'll give you the abbreviated version. Have you figured out Jack is my mom's stepson?"

"I thought so. He calls her Sarah."

"Which pains her no end. His mother left when he was a toddler and nobody knows where she is. But Nick and I grew up thinking that Sarah was our mom."

"She's not?" Now there was a shocker. "But you two look so much alike!"

"That's because she *is* my mom, but not Nick's. Nick just recently found out his mother was someone my dad had a brief affair with, before he met Sarah. Nick's mom left town and never contacted Dad about the pregnancy."

Morgan had to readjust her thinking quickly. She'd pictured the Chance family as perfect in every way, but apparently they had secrets like everyone else. "So where is his mother now? It's not Pam, is it?"

"No, Pam's his aunt, something we also just found out. His mother, Nicole, died when Nick was a few months old. She'd left instructions that if anything happened to her, Nick should be taken to my dad, so suddenly here was this baby on the doorstep when Sarah was pregnant with me. So they raised Nick to think Sarah was his mom, too."

"How does Pam figure in?"

"She kept track of Nick, her nephew, without him knowing she was doing it. She never had kids, so after her divorce she moved here to be close to him, but she kept quiet until all this came out last month."

"Wow."

"Yeah, it sucks. Supposedly my dad thought it would be better for Nick to think Sarah was his biological mother. Personally, I think he was covering his ass. He didn't like to admit he'd had unprotected sex and made some woman he barely knew pregnant."

"Your father was a complicated man, wasn't he?"

Gabe nodded. "That he was. And here we are at the edge of the trees. Just a little ways in and you should start hearing the creek."

But the first thing Morgan heard was the whine of a mosquito. She swatted at it and missed. "Should we haul that repellent out of your saddle bag?"

"Let's get there first. I have a plan." He slapped his cheek where a mosquito had landed.

"Your plan better be good." She smacked another one. "They're eating me alive."

"It's because we're in the forest. It's their hangout."

Morgan smacked her ear when she heard the tell-tale whine and now her ears were ringing. "So I've noticed."

But discounting the mosquitoes, which was tough to do, the forest was breathtaking. She spotted a rainbow of wildflowers scattered among ferns and vines. Lemon-yellow butterflies danced through the trees, and dragonflies fluttered their translucent wings as they buzzed past her.

"Do dragonflies eat mosquitoes?" she asked.

"Yes, as a matter of fact."

"Then we could use a squadron of them ASAP."

"We're almost there. Can you hear it?"

"No. I deafened myself when I slapped a mosquito."

Gabe rose on his stirrups and pointed. "It's right there. Through the trees."

She looked, and sure enough, sunlight flashed on the stream as it tumbled over smooth stones and cascaded down a waterfall about three or four feet high. Below the miniature falls swirled a pool, and beside it lay an intimate-looking crescent of sand. The gurgle of water, which she could actually hear now, welcomed them as they guided the horses down an incline to the creek.

Gabe dismounted and looped Finicky's reins over a tree branch. Pulling a blue-and-white checked blanket from his saddle bag, he shook it open and spread it on the sand. Then he took out the mosquito repellent and studied the label before setting that on the blanket.

"This is not looking like such a good plan, after all, Gabe. I can see the mosquitoes tying on little bibs."

"It's a great plan." He tossed a condom packet on the blanket before walking over to where she waited on Top Drawer. He held out his arms. "I'll help you off, and once you're on the blanket, you can strip down."

She drew back in horror. "Strip down? Are you nuts? I'm not exposing any more flesh than necessary to these vampires!"

"I'll be right there with the repellent. This'll work."

"What? You're going to spray it all over my naked body?"

"Uh-huh. I read the label, and it'll be fine. You might want to close your eyes, though." He motioned for her to come into his arms. "Don't be a wimp, Morgan. I promise I'll make it worth your while. But we have to work fast."

She gazed at him and shook her head in wonder. "You are truly insane, Gabriel Archibald Chance."

"Yeah, and that's why this will be so much fun." He tipped back his Stetson and gave her the sort of cocky grin that could make a woman agree to all sorts of foolish schemes, including having sex while mosquitoes swarmed.

"Okay, but you have to promise to scratch my back all night if I need you to." She leaned toward him.

"Sweetheart, it will be my pleasure." He swung her off the horse as if she were a feather and set her on the blanket. "Now, strip! Fast!" He picked up the can.

She started with her boots and hat, but once she took off her shirt, she realized that speed was truly of the essence. The quicker she moved, the less time those little buggers had to get a bead on her. In no time she was standing naked on the blanket. "Spray me, Gabe!"

"You got it!" He aimed the can.

As he sprayed, she twirled, holding out her arms and dancing on the blanket in case any mosquitoes had made it through the mist.

"That should do it." The can dangling loosely in his grip, Gabe stood for a moment just looking at her.

"What? It's not like you haven't ever seen me naked before."

"I haven't seen you dancing naked in the sunlight next to the creek in my favorite makeout spot. That's a sight to behold."

"This is your favorite spot?"

"Since high school."

"So you've brought other girls here?" She wasn't crazy about that idea. So far she'd been part of several firsts with him and she'd like to keep that streak going.

He seemed to realize she wasn't happy about being taken to the same rendezvous point he'd used for his other dates. "Well, yes, but not in the daytime. And definitely not when the mosquitoes are around."

Morgan laughed. "Now I feel special." She held out her hand and wiggled her fingers. "Can, please. Your turn, nature boy."

Watching Gabe rip off his clothes was almost worth getting bitten by mosquitoes, but to her relief, they weren't landing on her, at least not yet. So she was free to admire the ripple of Gabe's pecs as he pulled off his shirt and dropped it to the ground.

A mosquito landed on his chest, and she reached over and slapped it.

"Ow."

"Oh, I'm so sure that hurt. Hitting you is like

smacking a piece of granite. You have such a hard body, Gabe." Sunlight burnished his chest hair, turning it to gold. She gave in to temptation and ruffled it with her fingers.

He caught her hand. "Back off, lady. I gotta finish this striptease before the skeeters attack again."

"Go for it." She stepped away, can at the ready.

Once he'd shucked his jeans and underwear to reveal what was going on under that confining material, Morgan concluded this plan of his might not be such a mistake, after all. Her body hummed in anticipation of having that gorgeous equipment deployed in the interests of her pleasure.

But first he had to be anointed with mosquito repellent. "Hold out your arms."

He covered his crotch with both hands. "Spray me like this."

She gazed at him. "I just allowed you to spray every inch of me with this stuff. Are you worried about getting some on your Johnson?"

"As a matter of fact, I am."

"Why? You said it was environmentally friendly."

"That doesn't mean dick-friendly. Your special parts are tucked away, but mine are right out there, and I don't care what the label says, I don't trust it not to… make me sterile or something."

She choked back a laugh. He was deadly serious about this, as most men were about their pride and joy. He wouldn't appreciate her amusement. And for all she knew, the bug repellent might sting his more tender parts. "You could've put on a condom first."

"No, because then spray could get on it, and I'm not

taking a chance with your special parts, which will soon come in direct contact with my special parts."

"You know, that's touching in a weird kind of way."

"Just spray me, okay?"

"You bet." She walked around behind him. Now there was a view. Mountains and wildflowers were nice and all, but she'd take a screensaver showcasing Gabe's buns any day.

His buns looked as tight as his pecs. She gave him a sharp slap there to check it out.

"Hey!"

Just as she'd thought. Satisfyingly firm. "Sorry. Mosquito." Then she began spraying because actual mosquitoes were showing up.

"That's good enough."

"But I'm not sure I got every—"

"I'll take my chances." He grabbed the can from her and tossed it on the ground. "You're torturing me."

"With mosquito spray? Now who's the wimp?"

"Not the spray, the jiggle." He pulled her into his arms and cupped one slightly sticky breast. "You were bouncing all over the place. I couldn't wait another second to get my hands on you. You feel so damn good, Morgan. No wonder the mosquitoes want to suck on you."

"But you'd better not. I probably taste awful."

"Probably." He ran his hands over her breasts, fondling them with obvious relish. "But I can touch. Before we go back, we'll take a quick dip in the creek." He slid his hands down to her waist. "Was there really a mosquito on my butt?"

"No."

"Then you deserve some payback." He gave her a swat on the rear.

"Hey!"

"I'd kiss it and make it better, but you probably taste like turpentine, so I'll have to settle for a tush massage instead." He began a slow kneading motion that stimulated all of what he referred to as her *special parts.* Soon she was breathing like a long-distance runner.

"Mmm." She closed her eyes and let her head fall back as he built the tension within her.

"Like that?"

"Uh-huh. But two can play at that game." Opening her eyes, she reached down between his legs.

He groaned. "So they can."

"Is this what you had in mind when you brought me down here?"

"We're getting closer to my vision."

She stroked and teased him until his balls began to contract and his penis was slick with moisture. "How's that?"

"We need that condom."

"Allow me." Stepping out of his arms, she knelt on the blanket and located the condom lying there. As she turned back to him, she was in the perfect position to slide it on, but she couldn't resist wrapping her hand around him first and nibbling a bit.

"Morgan…"

"You didn't get sprayed there. You taste delicious."

"You're playing with fire."

"No, I'm playing with your magnificent pe—"

"Put the condom on." He spoke through clenched teeth. "Please."

"Okey-dokey." She was trembling a bit from excitement and fumbled the job, but finally managed it.

Grasping her by the shoulders, he hauled her to her feet and covered her mouth with his in a kiss filled with desperation. Then he drew back, panting. "I need you on your back on that blanket, Morgan. And no fooling around."

His urgency thrilled her to her bare toes. She cradled his face in both hands. "Somebody's a wee bit tense."

"And somebody has the remedy between her soft thighs. On the blanket, Morgan."

"Next time I get to order you around." But secretly she liked his take-charge attitude. When it came to sex, commands could be exciting.

Crouching down, she sat on the blanket and then stretched out. The sand crunched underneath her and she wiggled a little on the blanket, molding the ground to her body. Then she gazed up as sunlight filtered through the green leaves of tree branches that arched over the tiny beach.

In the time it took her to draw one quick breath, Gabe was there. Bracing his arms on either side of her shoulders, he probed once and then thrust deep with a growl of satisfaction.

Morgan sighed with pleasure and wrapped her arms around him. Then she wrapped her legs around him for good measure. Even when they were both sticky with mosquito repellent, being naked with Gabe had become her favorite thing. The connection was magic, and would, in a few moments, become transcendent.

Except for the mosquito that had just landed on Gabe's shoulder.

"Gabe, there's a mosquito on your—"

"Don't care." His eyes were twin flames of blue as he eased back and pushed forward again. "Nothing matters but this."

11

Nothing matters but this. The words seemed to echo through the forest as Gabe looked into Morgan's eyes and began the age-old mating rhythm that he craved with every ounce of his being. He'd never been so focused in his life, and that was saying something for a guy accustomed to fierce competition.

When Morgan came, arching upward with a joyous cry, happiness surged through him because he'd given her pleasure. Then his own orgasm ripped through him, narrowing his world to this time, this woman, this driving need to be joined with her.

For long seconds he was blind and deaf to his surroundings as his body absorbed the shock of that climax. But gradually the shudders grew less and he became aware of sunlight on his back, the loamy scent of new growth and water sliding over stones.

He looked into Morgan's eyes and found lazy contentment there, which pleased him. But her blue-green gaze was filled with something more, something tender and new. He wondered if she knew how much she was allowing him to see, and how vulnerable that made her. His chest grew warm, as if someone had covered him with a soft blanket. Just like that, their relationship moved beyond lust into territory that Gabe hadn't traveled much in his adult life.

He should be worried about that, but he couldn't bring himself to worry when the air smelled of evergreens and great sex. Leaning down, he brushed his lips over hers. "Ready for a dip in the creek?"

"I'll bet it's ice-cold."

"Yep." Leaving her warmth, he divested himself of the condom. He'd deal with it later, after they'd washed off the sticky repellent.

"We don't have towels."

"We'll use the blanket. Up you go!" He scooped her into his arms.

"Gabe! I can get myself in."

"Ah, but will you?" He carried her to the edge of the pool and sucked in a breath as he stepped into the water. He wasn't even sure he could do this, but they both needed a good dunk.

"I heard that! I heard you gasp. If it's that cold, then I'm not going in." She tried to wiggle out of his arms.

"Yes, you are, and so am I." He waded into water cold enough to freeze his nuts. "Stop struggling, or…" He lost his footing and they both went down, accompanied by her ear-splitting screech of dismay and his pungent swearing.

He scrambled to his feet and stood in waist-deep water. He could feel his privates shriveling in protest. Morgan faced him, her mouth open in a silent scream as water streamed down her face from her dripping hair. Her chest was heaving, which was a bonus, and her nipples were puckered into tight little raspberries. Cold as he was, Gabe enjoyed seeing that.

Figuring the best defense was a good offense, he grinned at her. "Refreshing, huh?"

She gulped in air. "*Refreshing?* Try hypothermia!"

"Ah, it's good for you."

"You think so? Then take this!" She splashed frigid water all over him.

"Two can play that game!" He splashed her back, and the war was on.

At some point during the battle Morgan started laughing, probably because she'd adjusted to the water temperature and the exercise had warmed her up. Gabe decided that it might be safe to advance in her direction without danger of being kneed in the groin, so under cover of myriad showers of water, he managed to get close enough to grab her.

She yelled and pretended to fight him off, but in the end she pulled his head down for a very wet kiss with lots of tongue involved. Apparently he was forgiven.

Caressing her water-slicked body gave him ideas for the future involving showers and possibly hot tubs. But if they didn't stop kissing like this, he'd have to do something more immediate to satisfy them both, and he wasn't willing to deal with mosquitoes a second time.

Reluctantly he lifted his mouth a fraction from hers. "We need to leave."

Her breath was warm on his lips. "Just like a man. Throws you in the water but won't let you stay." Beneath the water, she fondled his cock, which was already growing rigid.

"Just like a woman. Complains about going in and complains about getting out." He should make her stop doing that, and he would...in a minute.

"Just like a man. His brain says go, but his dick says stay."

He had a tough time arguing with that. He should end this maneuver while he could still walk. Ah, but her touch was heaven.

"How're you feeling?" she murmured.

"Rooted to the spot."

"Good. 'Cause I want that blanket first." Letting go of his penis, she splashed her way toward the beach and was wrapped in blue-and-white checks before he could take his next breath.

"You set me up!"

"Payback!" she sang out.

She looked so smug that he couldn't help laughing. Maybe he'd had this much fun with other women, but if so, he couldn't remember. This relationship was quickly taking center stage in his life, the very place that used to be occupied by cutting-horse events. Now there was a startling insight.

And maybe it was no coincidence that Morgan was suddenly so important to him. He'd allowed Jack to side-track his plans and Morgan had come along soon after. By distracting himself with Morgan, he avoided having to challenge Jack. That was not good, not good at all.

MORGAN HAD BEEN so busy drying off and dressing quickly to ward off the mosquitoes that she hadn't paid much attention to Gabe. He'd seemed pretty busy doing the same, so they hadn't taken time to make pleasant conversation. While he dressed, she'd waved her borrowed hat to keep the mosquitoes away. They'd managed to ride back through the woods and into the meadow without getting bitten more than a few times.

But once they were in the meadow, Morgan could tell that something was bothering him a lot more than a few mosquito bites. Being a direct sort of girl, she decided to ask him about it. "Are you upset because I abandoned you in the water?"

He smiled at her, the first time he'd done that since climbing out of the pond. "Nope. It was funny."

"Then what's wrong?"

His sigh seemed to come from somewhere deep inside. "As you've probably been able to tell, I've loved every minute of being with you these past two days."

Uh-oh. This was how guys started a kiss-off speech. She told herself not to panic, but panic was exactly what she felt. Even though she wasn't interested in a permanent commitment, she'd still allowed herself to become invested. And now he sounded ready to change the game.

"If it's your mother's matchmaking that's bothering you, I can fix that," she said. "I won't spend any more time at your place, and I probably shouldn't be riding your horse, either. She's reading far too much into it."

"It's not my mother. It's me. I've devoted the past ten years of my life to honing my skills in the arena. Every summer I've competed, and every winter I've trained to get even better. I eat, sleep and dream competition.

It's all I've cared about since I graduated from high school."

"I admire that kind of intensity."

He gazed at the Tetons outlined against the blue sky. "So do I, and I've lost my edge."

"Lost it? Since when?"

He turned to her. "This summer. And the thing is, I was worried about my slump, but the more I'm with you, the less I care about it."

"Wait a minute." Her sense of justice prevailed. "That's been all of two days. And it's not as if I've been hounding you for attention, either. I didn't plan to see you until tonight. You're the one who called and asked if I'd come out to the—"

"Hey, hey, I know. I said this was my deal. You haven't done a thing except be your wonderful, sexy self. I'm the one who's allowed this to become an obsession that's taking my mind completely off riding."

A sick feeling settled in the pit of her stomach. If he was losing focus, it didn't matter whether she'd caused that to happen or not. She would still be labeled as the reason, the fly in the ointment, the glitch in the plan. The bottom line was that with her around to tempt him, he would lose his motivation to do what he'd spent all those years training for.

"Gabe, if you need to get back out there and compete, then go! I'll be the first one to push you out the door. Hell, I'll push you out and lock it behind you!"

He angled Finicky so that the two horses almost touched before pulling back on his reins. "Let's stop a minute. This isn't the kind of conversation we should have when I can't touch you."

"Isn't that the crux of the problem? You can't keep your hands off me?"

"No, that's not the problem. Touching you is a privilege and I love doing it." He reached for her hand.

"Back off, cowboy." She guided Top Drawer a short distance away. "You've made me feel like Typhoid Mary. You can talk from over there."

He groaned in obvious frustration. "I'm not saying this right. The problems began before I met you and came to a head when I left the circuit to bring home an injured horse."

"Doozie."

"Yes. I've stayed home to take care of her, but now Jack's questioning whether I should go back out on the circuit…ever."

"Is it up to him?"

"Technically he controls the finances." Gabe scratched his shoulder.

Morgan remembered the mosquito that had landed there when they were making love. The way this discussion was going, they wouldn't be doing that again soon.

"But I own a fourth of the ranch," Gabe added, "and I could use that as leverage."

"And force the issue. Now that I've met Jack, I can't see that turning out well."

"Doesn't matter. Either I want this enough to fight for it, or I don't deserve to be out there."

"And you want to be out there."

He gazed at her, his blue eyes troubled. "It's been my whole life, Morgan. And Top Drawer has a shot at the Hall of Fame if I can get my act together and win more prize money on him. He has the heart and the ability. He just needs me to focus better."

"The Hall of Fame sounds like a big deal."

"It is."

"I'm beginning to see why your mother thought it was so significant that you loaned me this horse. What in hell were you thinking, letting me ride him?"

"I don't regret that for a minute." He paused. "But you're right. Loaning him to someone I barely knew wasn't very smart. Still, if I hadn't done that, we wouldn't have enjoyed these past two days together."

She swallowed. "It's clear that you need to call a halt, though. Get your life on track." She sounded a little gruff, and she couldn't help that. He'd taken her into the candy store, let her taste some of the best truffles, and now it was over. She was allowed to be disappointed.

"I'm thinking so," he said gently. "Sorry."

"That's okay, Gabe. Truly. All either of us wanted was a romp, and that's exactly what we've had. No regrets." Or none that she'd admit to while he was around. "We need to get back to the ranch or they'll wonder what's happened to us." She nudged Top Drawer into a walk.

"Mom will still want you to stay for dinner." He brought Finicky alongside her.

"Thanks, but I don't think that's a good idea. For one thing, I'm a mess." For another, she wouldn't be able to eat a thing, knowing that he would soon confront Jack. If he succeeded in getting what he wanted, he'd be gone for the rest of the summer.

Although she might kid herself that they'd reconnect in the fall, she doubted it. Once he'd labeled her a distraction from his chosen path, he wouldn't want to risk hooking up with her again.

"Damn it, Morgan. I didn't mean to hurt you."

"Oh, you didn't!" She plastered on a smile to prove it. "I'm a lot tougher than that. I'd rather not stay for dinner, all things considered, but I'll take the brownies, if that's okay."

"Oh, yeah. I forgot all about the brownies and coffee."

"I wonder why." She turned and winked at him, to further make the point that she was still the same wild and crazy girl who could tease him about the sex they'd shared. It would take more than this to break her heart, yessiree.

GABE HATED the way he'd had to leave things with Morgan. She'd taken the brownies, but she hadn't wanted a tour of the barn. He could hardly blame her under the circumstances.

As he'd helped her off Top Drawer and held her for that brief moment before her feet touched the ground, he'd wondered what the hell he was doing sending her off like this. She was his fantasy come true. He'd never had it so good.

And that was the problem. He could easily see himself filling the rest of the summer with hot sex. How could a guy complain when he had a willing Morgan in his arms?

So he'd loaf all summer, doing odd jobs around the ranch and spending his spare time with Morgan. Gradually he'd lose his will to compete. Cozy winter nights with her could convince him not to train quite so hard.

By next summer, if Jack continued to complain about the expensive entry fees, Gabe would probably give up competing altogether. After all, he'd have Morgan to comfort him.

While part of him longed for that, mostly the part below his belt, his brain and heart would always wonder if he'd sold out, if he'd let his big brother determine his future instead of taking the reins himself. He wouldn't have to wonder that now, though. As he unsaddled the horses and brushed them down before putting them back in their stalls, Jack walked out of the barn. Showtime.

Jack propped his hip against the hitching post and took off his black Stetson. He pretended to examine his hatband. "How did Morgan like her tour of the ranch?"

"Okay. But I have something else I need to discuss with you." Gabe finished up and tossed the brush into the plastic caddy they used for the grooming tools. He turned to Jack. "I'm going to assume that Doozie will be fine by the end of the month. I plan to enter Top Drawer in every cutting event I can find in August, to make up for the layoff."

Jack put on his hat and adjusted the brim. "It's a waste of money, Gabe. I did a little research, and we've only had one sale this summer as a direct result of your contacts on the circuit."

"You can't judge it like that." Gabe held on to his temper, determined to take the high road. "If Top Drawer makes the Hall of Fame, that'll be huge for the Last Chance horses. I might still have time to do it this year."

"Maybe, maybe not. I don't think it's a good use of ranch resources."

Tightness traveled from Gabe's jaw through his temples and down the back of his neck. He flexed his fingers. "Are you saying you won't approve the expenditure?"

"That's what I'm saying. It's not in the budget."

Although Gabe desperately wanted to tell Jack where he could shove his precious budget, he kept his voice level. He wanted to stay cool as he delivered the next part. "Then we may have to get the lawyer involved."

Jack met his gaze. A dark and dangerous light flashed in his eyes. "The lawyer?" he asked quietly.

"Yeah, Jack, the lawyer. The guy who drew up Dad's will and then read it to us while we all sat in Dad's office the day after the funeral."

Jack pushed away from the hitching post. "Are you challenging my right to run the ranch the way I see fit? Because the will clearly states that Dad gave me that job."

"He also gave each of us an equal share of the ranch—you, me, Nick and Mom. I plan to use my one-fourth share to finance Top Drawer's entry fees."

"Impossible. The assets aren't liquid. We'd have to sell…" Jack's eyes narrowed. "This is that real estate agent's idea, isn't it?"

"Morgan? This has nothing to do with her."

"The hell it doesn't! You spend the afternoon traipsing around the ranch with her, and now you tell me that we have to sell off some of the acreage to finance entry fees. Any idiot would be able to put that together."

"You're wrong. In fact, she's bowing out of my life

so that I can focus on making this Hall of Fame thing happen."

"Bullshit! She wants a piece of the action!"

Gabe wanted to hit him. He could imagine how satisfying that would be, to knock that know-it-all expression off his face. "You are so full of it, Jack. I'm not even planning to see Morgan anytime soon."

"Tell that to someone who believes it. She's got you wrapped around her little finger. All she has to do is wiggle her—"

"Careful, Jack." Gabe's hands curled into fists. "Your mouth is about to get you into some serious trouble."

Jack went into a crouch and motioned with both hands. "Bring it on, baby brother. Bring it on."

Gabe mimicked Jack's stance. The guy had taught him how to fight. Gabe was about to show his teacher how much he'd learned. "With pleasure."

"Hello, boys." Emmett Sterling rode up and dismounted, not looking at them as he looped the reins around the hitching-post rail. "I figured you two might be inside getting ready for the big farewell dinner for Dominique."

Gabe glanced at Jack, who straightened and shrugged.

"Gabe, if you'll unsaddle my horse, I'd appreciate it," Emmett said. "Jack, come on in the barn for a minute. I think we have some dry rot going on and I want your opinion as to whether we need to tackle it first thing in the morning. Then we all need to get up to the house before Mary Lou pitches a fit."

"Sure thing, Emmett." Jack walked past Gabe, his thumbs shoved casually through his belt loops as if he didn't have a thing on his mind except checking out dry rot.

"Later," Gabe said in a low voice.

"Anytime, son," Jack murmured. "Anytime."

12

"WHERE'S MORGAN?" Gabe's mother pounced on him the minute he appeared in the small family dining room adjacent to the one they used when they were feeding the hands or entertaining a big crowd.

"She asked me to tell you how sorry she was to miss this." Gabe made it up as he went along. "She's not feeling well, and she decided to leave in case whatever she has is contagious."

Jack held the chair for Sarah. "I'd be willing to bet it's contagious," he said. "If I were you, Gabe, I'd monitor myself. You could be coming down with it, too."

Sarah glanced at Gabe in surprise. "It must have come on quick. She looked fine this afternoon."

"That was before she took a gander at the ranch," Jack said as he sat down. "Gabe, maybe you should tell Sarah what you told me, about contacting the lawyer."

"It's not a good time to discuss that." Gabe glared at his brother. They had a score to settle, but they weren't going to do it at the dinner table.

Gabe's mother sighed. "Jack, I really think, especially now, that you could call me Mom instead of Sarah."

"Yeah, Jack." Nick helped Dominique into her chair. "It's time."

"I'll add my vote." Pam Mulholland was seated next to Emmett.

Gabe hadn't thought about it before, but he suspected his mother of matchmaking between Pam and Emmett, too. Come to think of it, they were about the same age. Pam looked as if she'd put extra effort into her appearance tonight. She'd done something different with her blond hair, sticking some fancy jewel things in it, and her light blue blouse showed off a bit of cleavage.

Emmett had taken time to wash up and get in a quick shave. His ears turned pink every time he glanced over at Pam, and Pam looked at him as if he were the last piece of fudge on the plate. Gabe wondered how long this attraction had been going on.

Emmett cleared his throat and looked across the table at Jack. "It would be a courtesy if you would do that for Sarah, son."

If Gabe hadn't been so angry with Jack, he might have felt sorry for the guy. Jack wasn't used to being chastised in front of the entire family. Well, it was his own fault.

"Oh, never mind." Gabe's mother unfolded her napkin and put it in her lap. "I guess it's not that important."

Nick glanced between the two of them. "I think it is. And I'm in a better position to understand than I used to be, Jack."

"I don't think so," Jack said quietly. "You grew up thinking Sarah was your mother, and just because you found out that wasn't exactly true, it doesn't really change anything. I grew up knowing that my mother is still out there somewhere."

Gabe couldn't stand seeing the pain in his mother's eyes. "No, she isn't. Your mother is right there. Sarah Chance is the only person who's ever loved you as a son. Her son. It's only right that you—"

"Are you lecturing me about what's right?" Jack pushed back his chair. "Aren't you the guy who brought a real estate agent on the property today?" He stood.

"Jack." Sarah put a hand on his arm. "Have a little faith in Gabe's judgment. If he says Morgan's not out to exploit her friendship with him, we should believe him. I want you to drop this prejudiced behavior."

Jack turned to her. "Then explain to me why, within minutes of her slinking away—"

"She did not slink away!" Gabe shoved back his chair.

"That's enough." Emmett stood. "If you two boys are determined to get into it, then you will take it outside."

"But we're having dinner!" Sarah stood, too. "I demand to know what's going on."

Jack threw down his napkin and left his seat. "I'll tell you what's going on. Gabe wants to sell off his share of the ranch."

"Damn it, I didn't say that!"

Jack pointed a finger at him. "You sure as hell did."

"Hey!" Nick leaped from his chair. "Cut it out! I

wouldn't blame Dominique if she changed her mind about marrying into this family, if we can't get through a simple dinner without yelling at each other!"

Jack protested his innocence and Gabe jumped in, determined not to let his brother spread any more lies. As they tried to outshout each other, a piercing whistle brought silence to the table.

Sarah took her fingers from her mouth.

Gabe hadn't heard that whistle in years. He'd forgotten his mother knew how to do it, but hearing it now brought back memories of the times she'd used that whistle to bring order when her boys got out of line.

Narrowing her eyes, she aimed a laserlike glance at each of her sons. "Jack. Nick. Gabe. Sit down."

Gabe sat, and he noticed that Nick and Jack did the same.

"All right. I don't know what is going on, and I don't want to know now. We can deal with whatever the problem is after dinner, like civilized people. We're celebrating an engagement tonight, and I expect all three of you to sit here and behave yourselves. Is that clear?"

Gabe nodded, as did Jack and Nick.

"Good." His mother picked up her wineglass. "Let's begin by toasting the happy couple. Here's to Nick and Dominique. May you have a long and happy life together."

Gabe lifted his glass along with everyone else at the table. But as he drank, he looked over the rim of his goblet to find Jack staring right back at him. The message in his brother's dark eyes was easy to read. *This isn't over.*

MORGAN THOUGHT about making a meal of brownies and a bottle of red wine she had in the cupboard, but in the end she didn't feel like being alone. Drinking wine and thinking about Gabe would probably produce nothing more valuable than tears, and she didn't feel like crying herself to sleep tonight.

One thing she was good at—most likely a world champion at—was saying goodbye. After all those moves as a kid—she'd stopped counting at thirty—she could leave a situation like nobody's business and soon be on to the next thing. The hollow ache she felt was probably hunger as much as sadness.

So she took a long, hot shower, styled her hair and walked over to Spirits and Spurs. Once there, she chose to sit at the bar instead of a table, because she was hoping to talk with Josie about ghosts. They didn't have to mention the Chance men. No point in wasting breath on those boys. Morgan was interested in ghosts.

A few people greeted her on her way over to a stool, and one couple invited her to join their table. She was gratified that someone offered, but not surprised. She was used to going into a town and making friends, and already she was on speaking terms with most of the merchants in town and quite a few of the residents.

Adding Pam Mulholland from the Bunk and Grub as a contact would be nice, but she could manage that on her own without the help of Sarah Chance. She didn't need Sarah, and she didn't need her son, either. He'd been a pleasant diversion for a couple of days, nothing more.

Picking an empty stool at the end of the bar near the cash register, Morgan climbed up on it and watched

Josie work. Her long blond braid swung as she clinked ice into glasses, poured whatever combination had been ordered and then garnished the drink with a flourish. If the real estate business didn't pan out, Morgan figured she should train as a bartender. She'd be good at bartending, which involved interacting with people as much as it did mixing drinks.

"Hey, Morgan." Josie placed a cocktail napkin in front of her. "What can I get for you?"

"Something new and different."

"How about a jolly rancher martini?"

"Uh, I don't think so." The thought of anything to do with ranching made her ill.

Josie gazed at her with a knowing expression. "Then maybe a Pain Killer?"

Morgan winced. "Is it that obvious?"

"Not to everyone, I'm sure. I'm a bartender and I pick up on stuff. Plus I'm another woman who's been run over by one of the Chance boys."

"That's a good way to put it. Run over."

Josie sighed. "I'm sorry. You two looked happy yesterday."

"Yeah, well." Morgan forced a smile and shrugged. "Easy come, easy go. And I swear I didn't come in here to talk about it. I came in to talk to you about ghosts."

"Cool! We can totally do that. Let me mix you your drink. You'll like it—dark rum, coconut rum, orange juice, pineapple juice."

Morgan nodded in approval. "Rum to help me forget and vitamin C to keep me healthy for when a new guy comes along. Sounds perfect."

"Something to eat along with that? You need to keep up your strength, you know."

"Spoken like a veteran of the Chance wars."

Josie rolled her eyes. "With the scars to prove it. How about a cheeseburger and fries? Comfort food works wonders at a time like this."

"Then I should probably have a chocolate shake to go with them."

Josie grinned and shook her head. "I've discovered the Pain Killer goes great with a cheeseburger and fries." She patted the bar in front of Morgan. "Hang in there, girlfriend. I'll be back in a flash with Dr. Josie's prescription."

Girlfriend. It sounded nice. Morgan had made friends in town, but she hadn't made what she'd call girlfriends, women she could hang out with, women with whom she shared secrets and beauty tips. That took time, and in a town this size, the cliques were pretty much formed in high school. Morgan hadn't lived here long enough as a teenager to be accepted into a group.

Josie's show of female solidarity was most welcome. Morgan wondered if Josie had a group of girlfriends, and if not, whether she'd like to start one with Morgan.

Within a couple of minutes, Josie set a sunny drink topped with a pineapple wedge on the cocktail napkin in front of Morgan. "Drink up. I put in your order for the burger and fries."

"Thanks, Josie."

"If you'll excuse me for just a sec, I have to get a refill for the couple at the far end of the bar."

Morgan suddenly wondered if she looked pathetic and needy. "Hey, I'm fine. You have a job to do. You don't have to babysit me."

"I thought you wanted to talk about ghosts?"

"Oh! I do!"

"Good." Josie grinned and launched into a Schwarzenegger version of "I'll be back" before hurrying to supply new drinks to the couple.

Morgan sipped her Pain Killer, which tasted like something she should be drinking next to a pool or on the beach. That image was way better than whatever might surface while she downed a jolly rancher.

Not that Gabe hadn't been jolly. He'd been a regular laugh riot until the moment he'd decided she was an impediment to his riding career. Damn it, anyway. She hadn't asked him to ride over and save her from Geronimo's antics.

In fact, she'd tried to talk him out of coming to her rescue. He'd been the one pursuing her until suddenly he stopped. To hell with him and the horse he rode in on. Literally.

She'd been fine before Gabe had arrived on the scene and she'd be fine now that he was about to take himself off to win more championships and get his horse inducted into the frickin' Hall of Fame. She didn't want what he was selling, anyway. He might pretend not to want commitment, but he was a Chance, a man with a legacy to uphold.

Considering the speed with which things had developed between them, she could end up married and pregnant before she knew what hit her. She was well rid of Gabe Chance. Well. Rid. Of. Him.

"Ready for another?" Josie appeared in front of her and gestured to the glass.

Morgan glanced down and was amazed to discover she'd finished off her Pain Killer. She was feeling pretty good, too. If Gabe Chance were to show up right now, she'd spit in his eye.

She met Josie's questioning gaze. "Sure, why not? I'm not driving. And this is a celebration."

"Oh?"

"I'm celebrating dodging a bullet."

"Gotcha." Josie took the empty glass and proceeded to make up another Pain Killer. "Let me check on your burger," she said as she delivered the second drink. "I'm caught up for a while, so we really will be able to talk about ghosts when I get back."

"Okay." Morgan wished now she hadn't allowed Gabe to hustle her out of the bar so fast after she'd seen the shimmering light. If she'd known he was going to dump her, she would have been less agreeable…about a lot of things.

"Here's your burger. Watch out. Plate's hot." Josie set it down next to Morgan's drink along with a napkin and silverware. "So, did you see something in here last night?"

"I think so." Morgan told her about the ghostly light that seemed to come through the front door and then park itself at the corner table next to the hallway leading to the bathrooms.

Josie's gray eyes lit up as the story progressed. "I've seen that same light! What happened after that? What did Gabe say?"

"He was in the bathroom and on his way out—he walked past it without noticing."

"But then he turned around and saw it, right? This is awesome. He won't be able to make fun of my ghosts anymore if he actually—"

"That's the frustrating part. I told him to turn around and look, but when he did, it was gone."

Josie's shoulders slumped. "Damn. He probably thinks you were pulling his leg."

"I don't think so. He had me out of here and walking down the street in no time. I think he was freaked out, although he kept insisting I'd seen car headlights coming through the windows."

"Are you saying he was scared?" Josie looked doubtful. "Big bad Gabe Chance?"

Morgan giggled. "I think he was terrified." For some reason she found that funny. "I figure if he'd actually seen that shimmering light he would have screamed like a girl."

"Amazing." Josie tapped her finger against her chin thoughtfully. "All along I thought the Chance boys were convinced I was making up the ghosts as a marketing ploy. Instead they might be nervous about coming face-to-face with one."

"I can't speak for the other two, but I'm convinced Gabe believes the ghosts are real. He doesn't want to admit that to himself or anybody else, but if he didn't believe in them, he wouldn't have been so quick to vacate the premises last night."

"Jack used to poo-poo the whole idea, too. I told him that the ghosts have been here all along, probably way before I bought the place."

"You think so?"

"It makes sense. Whoops. Here comes another order. And you need to eat your food before it gets cold." Josie went to the end of the bar and took a slip from the waitress.

Morgan tucked into her burger, which tasted great. Either the Pain Killers had worked or she wasn't all that torn up about Gabe, because her appetite was fine. And she was having fun talking about ghosts with Josie. Maybe the two of them could become a ghost-hunting team.

By the time Josie came back, Morgan had eaten most of her burger and about half of her fries. "So you think the ghosts have been here for years?"

"I do." With a damp rag Josie wiped down the bar, then leaned on it. "This has been the local watering hole for a long, long time. The building we're in now is close to a hundred years old, but from looking at old pictures of the town, I've decided there was another bar on this site even earlier."

"Do you think the people you bought from knew about the ghosts?" Morgan popped a fry in her mouth.

"Oh, yeah. But you don't tell a prospective buyer that the building they're about to purchase is haunted. They had no way of knowing that would have made the deal more exciting for me."

Morgan smiled at her. "I think it's cool that you're okay with the ghosts. Too bad Gabe isn't."

"It's a shame. He's probably related to at least two of them who come in here after hours. The more I think about it, I'll bet that's the very reason he doesn't want to confront one. A nameless ghost is one thing, but if it's somebody you knew…"

"Then it turns into a version of Dickens's *A Christmas Carol*. I can see why that might be scarier, but I still think it would be fascinating. Oh, well. Gabe's loss."

Josie nodded. "And that goes double when it comes to you, girlfriend. Gabe has really lost out there."

"I appreciate that." Morgan felt all warm and cozy again. "Jack obviously didn't realize what he had, either."

"Nope, he sure didn't." Josie straightened. "And with the way he's acting lately, I figure I dodged a bullet, too."

Morgan held up her hand. "High five!"

"Chick power!" Josie slapped Morgan's palm and grinned. "Who needs those Chance boys, anyway?"

"Not us, that's for sure." Morgan drained the last of her Pain Killer and set the glass down with a solid clunk. She felt like wiping her mouth with the back of her hand, but she didn't. If she'd had a pair of six-shooters strapped around her hips, she would've twirled them before shoving them back in their holsters.

Gabe Chance better not show his face around her door again, although she almost wished he would just so she could give him a piece of her mind. And a piece of her mind was the only thing she'd be giving him from now on. That was guaran-damn-teed.

13

SOMEHOW they all survived the meal, although Gabe had trouble eating with the knot of anger tightening in his gut. It was bad enough that Jack had accused him of trying to sell off part of the ranch without hauling Morgan's name into it. She was completely innocent, but Jack was determined to make her into some greedy opportunist.

Talk centered mostly on the house that Nick wanted to build and where the best site for it would be. Jack participated in the discussion with enthusiasm and never missed a chance to shoot a disdainful glance in Gabe's direction. The implication was clear—while Gabe was trying to carve a chunk out of the ranch, his brother Nick planned to increase its value by building a home for himself and his new bride.

After dessert and coffee, which Gabe thought dragged on far too long, Nick announced that he was taking Dominique for a moonlit walk to discuss house plans. After they excused themselves, Pam expressed interest in seeing how Calamity Jane's foal Calamity

Sam was doing, so Emmett offered to take her down to the barn and show off the ranch's newest resident. Before Emmett left, he leaned down and murmured something to Sarah.

She nodded before facing Gabe and Jack over a table scattered with the remains of their meal. "Emmett said I should holler if I needed any help with you two, but I trust that won't be necessary." She pushed back her chair and stood. "I want both of you to join me in Dad's office."

As she led the way down the hall, Gabe followed. Jack, obviously not wanting to bring up the rear, walked alongside him. Gabe sneaked a glance at him, but his brother was staring straight ahead, so he did the same. The walk to the office had an eerie *Green Mile* feel to it.

Gabe thought the choice of venue was a brilliant move on his mother's part. The office was relatively small and had become a sanctuary ever since his dad's death. Nobody would dare start a fist fight in there.

For one thing, it would be disrespectful. For another, there was too much chance of breaking something, like the green antique banker's lamp his mother had found for his dad several years ago, or the framed picture of all five of them taken at Jonathan Chance's sixtieth birthday bash at Spirits and Spurs.

Hard to believe that was only four years ago—before Jack became involved with Josie, before the fateful day of the rollover, before Nick found out Sarah wasn't his biological mother and that their neighbor Pam was his aunt. Now they'd lost one member of the family and were about to add another—Dominique.

Gabe was sorry Dominique had been there to hear the argument between him and Jack, but she probably needed to be aware that everything wasn't roses around the Last Chance these days. She should know what she was getting into. From what he'd seen of Dominique, she'd be able to handle a little strife without whining.

He didn't want to think about Morgan right now, but she popped into his mind, anyway. That woman wasn't a whiner, either. He'd figured that out back in high school when she'd accepted her parents' lifestyle without complaint. But she was no pushover. Moving here and setting up a business had taken guts. He admired that.

His mother sat down in his dad's oak swivel chair, positioned behind the desk, and motioned for Gabe and Jack to take the two chairs in front of it. She folded her hands on top of the old battle-scarred antique that had belonged to Archie Chance before it became Jonathan's.

Then she studied each of them in turn. "When your dad was alive, he was fond of taking whoever was fighting out to an empty corral and letting them go at it. I'm tempted to do that now because I'm so frustrated with both of you."

"Fine with me." Jack started to get up.

"Not so fast, Jonathan."

Gabe blinked. Nobody ever called Jack by that name, but it was his name, although he had a Junior attached. Their mother seldom did things for no reason, so Gabe decided she'd used that name on purpose to remind Jack whose boots he was standing in.

Jack sat down again.

Sarah cleared her throat. "I never thought beating each other to a bloody pulp proved anything except who'd been working out on the weight bench. Personally, Jack, I think you might want to reconsider challenging your little brother. He's bulked up a lot since you last whipped his ass."

Gabe started to laugh and thought better of it.

"The thing is, your dad is not here," his mother continued. "And although I miss him every day, I'm glad he wasn't here tonight. If he'd heard that kind of yelling from his boys at the dinner table, he would have taken you both on himself."

"You're right," Jack said. "I apologize for that."

Gabe nodded. "I apologize, too."

"But I won't take back what I said," Jack added. "I wish you'd been there when Gabe came in from his ride with that real estate agent. I wish you'd heard firsthand what he said."

Gabe was determined to stay calm, for his mother's sake. He turned to his brother. "Jack, you're twisting it so it sounds like something else. And you'd better leave Morgan out of this, or—"

"How can I? You came up with this demand immediately after spending time with her. She obviously suggested that—"

"She did not!"

His mother slapped a metal paperweight down on the desk. "Stop that, both of you. Gabe, tell me what you said to Jack that has him so riled up."

"I told him I was going back to my cutting-horse competition next month to give Top Drawer a chance at the Hall of Fame. Jack refused to pay for it. I said that we'd have to get the lawyer involved, because I have a quarter interest in the ranch, and I want to use my share to pay for entry fees and expenses."

"Which means selling off acreage!" Jack shouted.

Sarah's eyebrows rose. "Does it, really, Jack? Are we living that close to the edge?"

"It's not the immediate expense of Gabe's entry fees, or his per diem for another month." Jack blew out a breath. "But I'm not convinced he's helping us sell horses, and that means his competition is an unnecessary drain."

Sarah studied the two of them before focusing on Gabe. "Did Morgan encourage you to pull out your equity in some way? Does she want to be the listing agent for some of our land?"

"No! This is totally my idea. I don't see how Jack can stop me from competing when I have one-quarter interest in the ranch. I'm just asking for my share so I can continue what I've done for ten years. Personally, I think it's a great advertisement for Last Chance paints and will be even better if Top Drawer is inducted into the Hall of Fame. But if Jack won't back me on that, I have to figure out an alternative."

Jack pointed a finger at him. "Don't pretend Morgan didn't put you up to it. You're just trying to protect her."

Gabe's mother sighed. "You know, Jack, it doesn't matter whether Morgan is involved or not. Gabe has the right to liquidate his share of the ranch if that's what he chooses to do. We can either sell off enough to give him the cash, or we can buy him out. That's how your father set it up."

Jack clenched his hands in his lap. "So what about it, Sarah? Can you come up with your share of the money to buy Gabe out?"

"I suppose, if I borrowed against the value of the ranch."

Jack turned to him. "You hear that? You're asking your mother to go into debt to finance your ego-driven needs. How does that feel?"

"I'm not asking anyone to go into debt." Gabe stared Jack down. "But I'm not going to give up a skill I've honed for ten years and deny Top Drawer his shot because you're too damned focused on the bottom line. That's not the way Dad ran the—"

"Don't you dare throw that in my face." Jack started out of his chair again.

"Stop it, both of you!" Sarah stood. "Jack, I've let you handle the books ever since Jonathan died because that's the way he seemed to want it. But I plan to spend tomorrow going over our finances to see if we can afford Gabe's entry fees and expenses."

Gabe rose to his feet. "Thanks, Mom."

"Don't thank me yet. I could end up siding with Jack on this. If I do, we'll have to call a family meeting and get Nick's input. But I will not have this kind of infighting among you boys."

Jack also came to his feet. "It started with the real estate agent."

"She has *nothing* to do with this!"

His mother folded her arms, a sure sign she was

finished with the discussion. "Gabe, please ask Morgan to come over tomorrow. Her name's been bandied about all evening, and I won't know the truth until I talk directly with her. I hope she can make it."

Gabe wasn't sure if he could deliver on that request, but he'd give it his best shot. "I'll ask her."

"And now, if you'll both excuse me, I'm going to brew a cup of peppermint tea and take it into my room with a good book. Good night." She smiled at each of them as she left the office.

Gabe looked over at Jack. "I think we're done for now."

"Oh, we're far from being done." Jack's jaw twitched. "But I love that woman, and I'm not going to cause her undue stress by cleaning your clock."

"If you love her so much, why in God's name can't you call her Mom?"

"You wouldn't understand."

"Try me."

"If I tell you, will you leave me the hell alone about it?"

"Yeah. Yeah, I will."

Jack's face tightened as if bracing himself for a blow. "Okay, then. When I was a little tyke, I learned how to say mama and dada, like every kid does. Dada worked out okay for me, but mama, not so much. The person I associated with that word cared so little about me that she ran off. For you, the word is loaded with warm fuzzies. For me, it's the label you put on somebody who doesn't give a damn. Why would I call Sarah by that name?"

It was a long speech for Jack, and he appeared

drained by it. Slapping his Stetson on his head, he turned and walked out of the office.

So that was it. Gabe wanted to call after him and beg him to confide all that to the woman he refused to call his mother. But Gabe had promised to leave Jack alone on the subject, and he would honor that promise. It would be tough, though.

Jack's explanation also made it hard to be furious with the guy. Whether Jack realized it or not, he'd just admitted to having a gaping wound that had never healed. Gabe had never viewed Jack as vulnerable before. It put a whole new light on things.

BY NINE-THIRTY that night, Morgan felt sufficiently buoyed up that she could walk home and face sleeping in the bed she and Gabe had cavorted in not so long ago. She'd already changed the sheets that morning in anticipation of more cavorting tonight. She'd even added a vase of wildflowers to the bedroom and a few scented candles.

Grabbing her handy butane lighter, she lit the candles. A girl could have atmosphere even if the man of her dreams…cancel that…the louse who'd dumped her, wasn't in residence.

A girl could have music, too. She flipped on the CD player, which she'd loaded earlier with mood music. The wail of a sax and the thump of a jazz piano filled her bedroom. That was more like it.

Undulating to the music, she danced over to her dresser, stripped off her clothes in time to the beat, and opened a drawer. There it was, a black silk negligée she'd bought in Jackson last year and had never worn. She'd been saving it for a special occasion.

This morning that special occasion had looked as if it would involve Gabe, but she'd guessed wrong on that score. So what? She'd wear it anyway. Taking it out of the drawer, she raised her arms and slid it over her head with a sigh of delight.

A twirl in front of the mirror attached to her closet door confirmed what she'd seen in the dressing room when she'd bought this number. The plunging neckline was made for a well-endowed chick, and the short skirt would tease a man to distraction. If Gabe could somehow know about the seductive possibilities he was missing, he'd eat his heart out. But he would never know.

The Pain Killers Josie had prescribed continued to sing in her blood, relaxing her to the point that she contemplated unpacking her vibrator and having a party all by herself. She was, after all, still on vacation until tomorrow morning.

The Fourth of July long weekend was the first one she'd taken off since she'd arrived in Shosone. She'd been working hard to jump-start her business. She'd combed the town for listings and had spent weekends at open houses. At night she'd updated her Web site and taken online courses on how to be a better saleswoman.

She'd focused so completely on her business that she still had a few unpacked boxes tucked in the hall closet, and her vibrator was in one of them. Time to dig out that little happy-making device now that Gabe Chance had flown the coop. She didn't need him to have fun.

Naturally, the vibrator was in the bottom of the last box she went through. By the time she came up with it, she'd littered the hallway with old CDs, stuffed animals left over from her childhood, a Rubik's cube, a Slinky, assorted flower vases, a few paperbacks and an old issue of *Playgirl*.

She flipped through the magazine and discovered none of the models made her quiver with lust the way Gabe did. Sure, they all had awesome equipment. A man couldn't be in *Playgirl* without that. But none of them had Gabe's cocky grin or brilliant blue eyes that could create sizzle in two seconds flat.

Oh, well. Tossing the magazine back into the box, she picked up the vibrator and switched it on to make sure the batteries still worked. She was thankful they did, because she doubted she had any spares.

Normally she'd put her junk back in the boxes instead of leaving it spread all over the hall floor. But that seemed a little anal considering she was holding a working vibrator and wearing a do-me-now negligée.

As she stood to walk back into her bedroom, her doorbell chimed. She paused as intuition kicked in. No one in town knew her well enough to show up at her door at ten o'clock at night.

But outside the town limits lived one person who might think he could get away with it. If so, he had another think coming. Vibrator in hand, she walked to the door and checked the peep hole just to be sure her hunch was correct. It was.

She threw open the door and stood there, her hip cocked as she tapped the vibrator against her bare thigh.

Speechless, Gabe stared at her. Taking a breath, he opened his mouth. Then he closed it again.

Two Pain Killers had awakened the smartass in her. "Hello, Gabriel. Looking for someone to blow your horn?"

14

GABE WASN'T SURE what he'd expected to find when Morgan opened the door, but certainly not this. Hell's bells, but she looked…he couldn't even find a word that would do her justice. One thing she didn't look, though, was happy to see him.

For one wild moment he wondered if she'd moved on to someone else already, but the vibrator, a flesh-colored piece of plastic about the diameter and length of a penis, told a different story.

Gabe didn't have much experience with these things, but he'd always thought a woman used one as a quick remedy to fill in the gaps between guys. He'd never pictured a woman making a big production out of it with a skimpy nightgown, music and scented candles, which he could smell even though he wasn't inside yet.

Naturally, seeing her like this turned him on beyond belief. He didn't think she'd begun her evening of self-stimulation, but knowing what she'd had in mind quadrupled his lust factor.

He'd told himself this would be a quick visit to pass on his mother's request and then he'd get the heck out of there. He'd told himself that despite the relatively late hour, he needed to let her know what had happened and why his mother wanted to see her.

Yeah, he could have called, but he wasn't sure she'd have answered the phone. Even if she had picked up, convincing her to come out to the ranch tomorrow would be difficult over the phone. A personal visit had seemed like the only answer.

But everything he'd told himself about this trip to town, every rationalization for being here, was a damned lie. He'd come because he wanted to see her. No, that was sugar-coating it. He'd shown up at her door because he craved everything she had to offer, especially in terms of sex, but emotionally, too.

Knowing how weak he was when it came to Morgan, he had no business being here and should leave immediately. Then again, he might not have to worry about compromising himself by going to bed with her. Judging from the way she was glaring at him, she wouldn't allow that to happen in the next million years.

She looked as if she'd like to beat him over the head with that vibrator. She was obviously pissed, and he could understand that. Apparently it didn't matter to him whether she welcomed him with open arms or not. Smiling or frowning, she was the most delicious woman he'd ever met, and he ached for her.

She kept tapping that vibrator against her thigh. "You'd better state your business, cowboy, before a neighbor drives by and gets the wrong idea."

"I need to talk to you." He tipped the brim of his hat up with his thumb. "How about it. Can I come in?"

"Depends." *Tap, tap, tap* went the vibrator. "How long will it take you to say what you have to say?"

"Not long, but as you pointed out, with you in that getup and me standing at your door, it looks like we're negotiating a price."

"All right." She stepped back and used the vibrator like an usher with a flashlight to motion him in. Then she closed the door and faced him. Once again she tapped the vibrator against her thigh. "Okay, talk."

"Could you put that damned thing down? You're making me nervous."

Instead of doing as he asked, she switched it on. "Oh, pardon me all to hell." She advanced on him, the buzzing vibrator poised like a dagger. "I would hate to make you nervous." She poked him in the chest with the thing.

That brief contact made him tingle, and it wasn't a bad feeling, sort of like buzzing his lips together. He had an instant picture of her sliding that gizmo between her legs, and he was hard as a rock.

And speaking of buzzing lips, hers were glistening because she'd just licked them—slowly and very deliberately while giving him the eye. She was vamping him on purpose.

He cleared his throat. "Stop it, Morgan."

"Stop what? Being me?" She poked him in the chest again with the buzzing vibrator. "You might as well admit the truth. I'm too much woman for you. You can't take it." She aimed the vibrator lower.

He grabbed the end of it before she reached her obvious target, the fly of his jeans. The humming length of plastic sent tingling sensations through his arm. "Quit fooling around."

"But that's what you're supposed to do with it, Gabe." She held tightly to her end. "You need to leave now so I can go back in the bedroom and start." She looked into his eyes. "And I will have as many...orgasms...as...I... want."

He'd swear the damned vibrator was short-circuiting his brain because he couldn't think at all. Or maybe it was lack of blood to his brain that had caused it to stall out. Listening to her talk about orgasms was putting a strain on his privates unlike anything he'd ever known before.

Her voice dropped to a low purr. "Or maybe you don't want to leave. Maybe you want to stay and watch."

With a groan of surrender, he let go of the vibrator and pulled her into his arms. His last rational thought before his mouth came down on hers was that he'd leave if she struggled.

She didn't struggle. Instead she kissed him back with the same brand of desperation roaring through him. For a few seconds her hand, along with the vibrator, was wedged between them. The muffled pulsing sent his jacked-up nerves into overdrive. Maintaining that essential mouth-to-mouth connection, he scooped her into his arms, and the vibrator—still buzzing—dropped to the carpet.

His hat fell off somewhere between the living room and the bedroom, and he let it go. All he cared about was keeping his mouth welded to hers until this was done, because he didn't want to talk. Talking would only confuse the issue. And the issue was simple—his cock, not some damned piece of buzzing plastic, should be deep inside her, making her come.

As he laid her on the bed, he followed her down, his tongue stroking the fruit-flavored recesses of her mouth. He knew that taste. She'd had at least one, maybe more than one, of Josie's famous Pain Killers.

No wonder she was waving vibrators and wearing black silk...and unbuckling his belt and unfastening his jeans. Cooperation was a beautiful thing. He reached one-handed for the condom box and hoped she hadn't moved it since last night.

It was still there, but he spilled the packets everywhere in his attempt to open it. Didn't matter. He got his fingers around one, and that was all he needed to complete this mission.

He placed the packet into her busy hands as he continued to demonstrate with his tongue what he had in mind once she had him ready to rumble. She wasted no time, which was good, because there wasn't a second to spare.

He needed her with a white-hot certainty that he'd never experienced before. He didn't care if the house caught on fire or a flash flood came through. He would have her, and he would have her *now*.

Once he felt the welcome glide of latex over his throbbing dick, he shoved aside whatever black silk barred his way and...heart pounding like a jackhammer...took her in one sure stroke.

Okay. This was what life was all about. Swirling his tongue in her mouth, he began to thrust. She responded by lifting to meet him.

With his jeans down around his knees, his belt

jangled each time they came together. The noise blended with the liquid slide of bodies in an ever faster cadence. A rhythmic sound rose from deep in his throat and kept time with the *slap, slap, slap* as he pushed into her and she pushed back.

Yet still he kept his mouth on hers, his tongue mimicking the movement of his surging hips. She dug her fingers into his buttocks. Then she whimpered and nipped his lower lip as she ground her pelvis into his.

He felt the first contraction squeeze his cock and picked up the pace, increasing the friction that would send her up in flames. Her lips rose up, arching into him as he gave her everything he had and she came, her keening sound of release muffled against his questing mouth.

His orgasm hit him with the force of a charging bull, knocking the breath from him. At last he lifted his mouth from hers. With a sound that was half gasp, half groan, he trembled in the aftermath of passion he hadn't known existed.

Dazed and humbled by the power of his need for her, he looked into her eyes. "I can't…be without you. I thought I could, but I can't."

She reached up and cupped his face, her gaze troubled. "Then I'm bad for you, just like you said."

"No. You're what I need." He leaned down and brushed her lips with his as he pushed deep. "This is what I need."

"You're not thinking straight right now. I admit I was angry when you blew me off today, but I don't want to be the reason you give up your competition."

"Why not? What better reason?" He kissed her

cheeks, her eyes, her hair. "Tonight I watched Nick with Dominique and you know what? I was jealous of their plans. They're picking a site for a house. They haven't talked about it, but I'm sure they'll have kids."

"That's nice for them." Morgan's voice was flat.

"It would be nice for us. You'd make a great mother."

"No, Gabe!" She struggled beneath him. "Let me up."

"What's the matter?" He rolled away from her as she scrambled out of bed. "Don't you want kids?"

"Not now! Not in the near future!" She cupped her silk-covered breasts. "As I mentioned this afternoon when your mother was doing the matchmaking thing, I'm no Earth Mother who can hardly wait to get pregnant and feed babies."

"Well, sure, you said that, but I thought you just meant you didn't want kids right away. I'm not talking about immediately."

"I don't know if I'll *ever* want children. I was the oldest of seven, which means I helped raise those kids. I'm not eager to change diapers anytime soon. And if I'm not fixated on babies, then why get married?"

His brain was spinning. "Well, *there's* a switch. I thought I was the one keeping us from making a commitment."

"I didn't think I needed to get specific about my feelings." She paced the length of the bedroom. "Until you showed up tonight and started talking about babies. That sends chills down my spine, Gabe."

"So what is it you want? I thought you wanted to put down roots."

"Which I'm doing! I bought this house. I'm settling into this community by building a business. I plan to stay here a long, long time, maybe for the rest of my life. That doesn't mean I want to get married or reproduce."

"That's... I mean, don't most women..."

"I don't know about most women, Gabe. I just know about me."

"Yeah, but when you were so eager to climb into bed with me just now, I thought—"

"That I wanted marriage and babies? I climbed into bed with you because it was a rush to know you couldn't resist me. My poor ego was bruised when you sent me away this afternoon, and now I feel tons better."

"I see. Glad I could be of help." Man, this was depressing as hell.

"Gabe, I also love having sex with you."

He glanced up to find her smiling at him. That was some consolation. She didn't want to marry him, but at least she liked the sex. "I love having sex with you, too, but..."

"But what?"

He studied her. "I'm not sure. Good sex has always been plenty for me." He took a deep breath. "Let me clean up a bit before we continue this. I'm not at my best when I'm hog-tied by my own clothes." He waved a hand at jeans that were half on and half off. He was still wearing his boots, for crying out loud.

"Sure. Take your time. I'll go turn off the vibrator." She walked out of the bedroom.

Gabe waited until she was gone before he headed into her bathroom. Once there, he leaned against the sink and stared into the mirror. What in hell was wrong with him? In effect, he'd proposed to Morgan. And she'd turned him down.

To his knowledge he'd never proposed to a woman in his life, not counting Cheryl Danbury in the second grade. Did he actually want to marry Morgan? He was afraid he did, which made no logical sense but resonated in his gut as the right move. How that worked with his campaign to get back into competition and take Top Drawer all the way to the Hall of Fame wasn't clear to him at the moment.

One thing was clear—he couldn't think worth a damn when he was with her. One whiff of her special scent, one glance into those blue-green eyes, one glimpse of her lush curves, and he wanted her in the most elemental way.

Maybe that's where this marriage and babies thing had come from. She stirred his need to mate. No woman had done that before, and he didn't know how to handle it. He needed distance and perspective, especially because she didn't appear to share his mating instinct.

Tucking in his shirt and zipping up his pants, he buckled his belt and walked out into the living room.

She sat in a brown leather easy chair in her black nightgown that so lovingly showcased her spectacular breasts. She was wearing his hat.

And he wanted her again. He wanted to have her right in that chair. He'd sit where she was sitting and she'd ride him, her legs hooked over the arms of the chair and her nightgown pulled down to her waist. She would be wearing his hat, and she would be calling his name as he guided her hips up and down, up and down.

"What is it?" she asked softly.

"You." He swallowed. "I've never..." He massaged the back of his neck and willed his erection to go away. "I've never wanted a woman this...much."

"I'm flattered."

"And I'm completely disoriented. But the man with the goat called while I was at dinner with my family." He realized he still hadn't delivered his mother's message. Talk about brain freeze.

"The goat for Doozie?"

"Right. I'm leaving first thing in the morning for Colorado to pick it up. I'll be gone a couple of days. I think a little time apart is a good thing for us right now."

She nodded. "I think so, too."

"But I have a big favor to ask in the meantime."

"Oh?"

He noticed she didn't immediately agree to whatever it was. Morgan was keeping her wits about her, which was more than he could say for himself. "My mother asked if you'd be willing to come to the ranch and talk with her sometime tomorrow. Whenever works for you."

"Why?"

Taking a deep breath, he filled her in on what had happened when he'd told Jack he was returning to the circuit. "Jack's positive you influenced me to demand my share of the ranch."

Her eyes snapped with indignation. "That's so unfair, especially when I've said so many times that I think your ranch needs to stay just as it is. You're not serious about asking them to sell off some of the land, are you?"

"Of course not." Yet in the heat of his argument with Jack, he'd thought about it. There was acreage they didn't use for much of anything. But to say that to Morgan would be the equivalent of blasphemy, so he didn't.

"Well, that's good. I'd hate to see chunks carved off and developed."

"Strange talk coming from a real estate agent."

She lifted her chin. "Maybe you've been hanging out with the wrong real estate agents. We aren't all ready to rape the land. Some of us believe in working with existing dwellings whenever that's possible."

"That would be a good point to make with my mom. She really wants to hear your side."

"Will she believe me?"

"I think she will. But I can't speak for Jack. He plays by his own set of rules."

Morgan nodded. "So Josie said."

Unease rippled through him at the thought of Morgan and Josie comparing notes on the Chance brothers. "I'm not like Jack."

She gazed at him without responding, but he could see the wheels going around in that fertile brain of hers.

"I'm not! He goes to extremes with things, like deciding to completely stop seeing Josie because he was in bed with her when Dad died. And now he's working himself to death and pinching every penny, which is the exact opposite of how he was before. Jack can't seem to do anything in moderation."

She stood and took off his hat. "Whereas you, on the other hand, do everything in moderation."

"Well, yes. Pretty much. Mostly."

"Your competition, for example?"

"That's not a good example. You have to go all-out if you want to get anywhere on the cutting-horse circuit. You can't make a half-assed attempt to compete."

"Or, as you put it this morning, you eat, sleep and dream it."

Gabe ran his hand through his hair. "Look, I can see where you're going with this reasoning, but I'm not like Jack. He gives single-mindedness a bad name."

"Okay." She held out his hat.

He took it and crammed it on his head. "I mean, maybe I've gone a little overboard when it comes to you, but that's understandable, too."

"Is it?"

"Sure. You're so much my type it's scary. You're like an all-you-can-eat buffet of my favorite foods."

That made her smile. "I guess that describes how I feel about you, too."

"Yeah?" He liked knowing that.

"Mmm. You're a true banquet, Gabriel Archibald Chance. An endless feast." She got that look in her eye, the one that made him forget everything except taking her back to bed.

He shoved back the brim of his hat. "You know, Morgan, it's not all that late. We could take a little time to head on down the buffet table again and load up our plates."

"No."

"No? But you just said—"

"I know what I just said." She looked into his eyes. "You may not be like Jack, but I am. And tonight I'm going to practice moderation, even if it kills me. Go home, Gabe."

15

SENDING Gabe home was one of the toughest things Morgan had done in a while. Driving out to see Sarah Chance the next morning came in a close second. Morgan wasn't guilty of the crass opportunism Jack had accused her of, but she *was* guilty of turning down Gabe's marriage proposal, or what had passed for one.

All the way down the long dirt road, she tried to convince herself that it hadn't been an actual proposal. Gabe had only said they could have kids and she'd be a great mother. That wasn't the same as pledging his undying love and begging for her hand.

Come to think of it, the word *love* hadn't been part of the discussion. Gabe had been honest about his unremitting case of lust, but the other *L*-word hadn't been mentioned. Sarah had said she wanted Gabe to find someone he loved passionately and who loved him back with equal passion.

Okay, then. Morgan didn't need to feel as if she'd stomped all over Sarah's dream of having her as the newest daughter-in-law candidate. Sarah wouldn't want any wedding plans that didn't come with buckets of love. Gabe didn't love her and she didn't love him.

She couldn't possibly love him. That would be totally illogical, against the laws of nature. They'd known each other for six months in high school and had only reconnected two days ago. Love took longer than that to develop. Everyone knew that.

But…she couldn't deny she'd had a major crush on Gabe in high school, or that she'd thought about him many times since then. She hadn't moved to Jackson Hole specifically because of Gabe Chance, but once she'd arrived in the area, she'd checked on his marital status.

Ever since coming to Shoshone, she'd hoped to catch a glimpse of him. She'd given up after discovering that he spent his summers out of town participating in cutting-horse competitions. But if she wanted to be brutally honest with herself, she'd known that he'd returned at the end of June, and she had hoped they'd run into each other during the town's Fourth of July activities.

If a person could be poised to fall in love, then she was in that category. And Gabe had proved to be gallant, funny, a good sport, a great dancer and a dynamite lover. Every time he popped into her mind, which was embarrassingly often, her heart fluttered. Every time they met, her heart raced. And when they were naked together, her heartbeat went totally off the charts.

Oh, hell. She was in love with him. How had that happened? And how could she make sure that nobody found out, especially Sarah, but most especially Gabe himself?

How embarrassing if he should figure out that she was in love with him, when all he felt was lust. How pathetic would that make her? Well, he wouldn't find out.

By the time she was eight years old, she'd perfected the art of pretending not to care. When her parents had repeatedly yanked her away from a place soon after she got comfy there, she'd learned to act as if it didn't matter. She'd use that skill to keep her secret.

The Last Chance was one gorgeous place, and since this might be the last time she drove out here, she took the time to admire the house as she approached. The gravel drive that circled around in front created an island of greenery anchored by two blue spruce trees. Their velvety branches swooped gracefully, as if gesturing toward the massive front door.

Judging from the height of the trees, which were taller than the house, Morgan guessed that Gabe's grandparents had planted them. This was a home built to welcome and house loving couples. No wonder that's what Sarah wanted for all her sons.

Speaking of Sarah, she sat on the porch in a rocker with another woman about her age. Although Sarah had chosen to leave her silken bob its natural white color, the other woman had opted for golden blond. Both women were dressed in jeans and checkered Western shirts.

Morgan was surprised to see someone else there. She'd expected Sarah would want to keep the discussion confidential.

If Morgan had to guess, she'd say the blonde with the curvy figure was Pam Mulholland from the Bunk and Grub. Both women stood when Morgan got out of her Grand Vitara and walked toward the front steps.

Sarah smiled as if greeting an old friend. "Hey, Morgan! Pam stopped by to see how our egg supply was holding out and I asked her to stay and meet you since last night didn't work out."

"I'm the egg lady," Pam said. "I've always wanted to keep chickens, and now, with the B and B, I can."

"And she's kindly agreed to sell her surplus to us. Did you bring business cards, Morgan?"

"I...uh, sure. I have some." Morgan never left home without her business-card holder, but she hadn't expected to haul it out this morning. She fished it from her purse as she mounted the porch steps.

"I guess a formal introduction isn't necessary," Sarah said. "Tell me, Pam, do you notice any horns growing out of Morgan's head?"

Morgan blinked. Apparently they were going to cut to the chase.

Pam didn't seem the least surprised by Sarah's direct comment. "No horns. But that's a beautiful shade of red hair, Morgan. I assume that came from the Irish side of O'Connelli."

"My looks are from my dad's O'Conner relatives and my personality is more from the Spinelli side." She handed Pam all the cards she was carrying and shifted into professional mode. "Thanks for taking these and recommending me. Do you like wine?"

"I'm a big fan of chardonnay. Why?"

"If you refer someone to me and they tell me so, I like to show my appreciation."

Pam nodded. "Sounds like an excellent business

practice." She looked closely at Morgan. "So I take it Jack thinks you're a real estate shark trying to sell the ranch out from under him?"

Sarah rolled her eyes.

"I guess Jack thinks that," Morgan said. "But I'm not—"

"Oh, we all know that," Sarah said. "Gabe is a good judge of character, and besides, yesterday before you came I called all my friends in town to find out what they knew about you. Everyone was extremely complimentary and assured me you weren't a greedy businesswoman."

"That's nice to hear."

Sarah nodded. "I was relieved, to say the least. In any case, I had to call this meeting so Jack will be convinced I've done due diligence on this issue."

"So you're not worried about my influence on Gabe?"

"My only concern is whether you and Gabe will figure out that you're madly in love with each other, or if you'll diddle around and screw it up."

Morgan's breath caught, but then she slipped into nonchalance like a suit of armor. "Goodness, we couldn't be in love. It's been all of two days."

"Sometimes that's enough. You weren't there last night to hear how Gabe stuck up for you when Jack wanted you tarred and feathered."

"I appreciate his doing that." Admittedly that gave Morgan a warm feeling, but she didn't dare attribute too much importance to it. Jack was on the outs with Gabe, anyway.

"I was in love with Jonathan after three days of

intense dating," Sarah continued. "And you can't deny there's a certain…intensity between you two." She smiled knowingly.

Pam sighed. "I wish I could borrow a little of that and sprinkle it over Emmett. If I weren't so crazy about him, I'd want to hit him upside the head with a two-by-four. But that's another whole subject."

"We can talk about that, too." Sarah motioned to the empty rocker beside her. "Come sit with us and enjoy the view, Morgan. We'll dish about men."

"I thought you wanted to hear my philosophy of real estate sales. Gabe said—"

"I'm sure he gave you pointers on what to discuss in order to make the right impression, but really, all I needed to see was your reaction to the baby pictures yesterday."

Morgan flushed. "I'm sure anyone would have thought they were cute."

"Maybe, but you lingered. And I watched your face. I'm a mother. I know these things. You're in love with him."

Feeling disoriented, Morgan managed a faint "I see."

"Anyway," Sarah continued, "I've asked Mary Lou to come out and bring coffee and her famous sticky buns. We may not be able to solve all the male-related problems around here, but if the four of us put our heads together, we might figure out what the hell to do about our biggest problem child, and that's Jack."

As Morgan struggled to regain her composure, Mary Lou arrived with a pot of coffee and her homemade sticky buns. Fortifying themselves with food and drink, the women proceeded to dissect Jack's behavior over the past nine months since his dad's death. Everyone agreed he needed to ditch the guilt and rejoin the human race.

Morgan quickly lost her self-consciousness among these wise and friendly women. She hadn't laughed so much in ages. For the first time since she'd moved to Shoshone, she truly felt a part of life here. Everyone else had been nice enough, but these three women accepted her in a way she hadn't experienced before.

She knew why that was, too. Sarah had given her the Chance stamp of approval. She had decided that Morgan and her son were in love with each other and it was only a matter of time before they figured that out and tied the knot. Morgan saw a million pitfalls in that scenario, but she wasn't going to spoil the mood on this beautiful morning.

Pam turned to Sarah. "Did Nick and Dominique settle on a site for the house before she left?"

"They're considering the spot where they first met. It's a rocky meadow, but they could use the rocks to build a beautiful fireplace. It's also far enough away that they'll have some privacy."

"And close enough that we'll get to spoil the grand-kids," Mary Lou said.

"Yeah." Sarah's expression grew dreamy. "Nick will make a great father. So will all the boys, in fact. Even surly Jack, once he finds the right woman."

Morgan would have loved to throw Josie's name into the conversation. She thought Josie had the backbone to deal with a guy like Jack. But Morgan wasn't about to launch a grenade into the middle of this cozy group. Besides, the topic of kids was a sensitive one for her.

Like it or not, any further relationship with Gabe was problematic. Granted, his sexual interest might eventually blossom into love. But she would be foolish to hope for that, because sooner or later the issue of children would become a bone of contention. Gabe would want them. His mother would long for them.

But Morgan just…didn't have any enthusiasm for the project. She especially didn't relish the idea of having babies while their father traipsed off to ride in cutting events. She wouldn't want to be the nag who insisted he stay home, but she wouldn't want to be the drudge left behind, either.

Better to end her association with Gabe and hope she could keep the friendship with Sarah, a woman she really liked. If Morgan planned to stay in Shoshone, she shouldn't get involved with Gabe unless she was prepared to go the whole nine yards, including babies. She wasn't willing to make that sacrifice.

But she'd rather not be the bearer of bad news. Gabe could tell his mother that Morgan was a great person but they weren't destined to be together. Sarah would take it better from her son, and perhaps Morgan could establish a relationship with Sarah the way she had with the mothers of other guys she hadn't married. This could work out.

If the thought of giving up a man she'd come to love drove a spike through her heart, she'd get over it. She'd grow and flourish in this town she'd chosen with or without Gabe Chance. Whatever else she was, she was a survivor.

GABE TOOK the ranch's single horse trailer to fetch Hornswaggled, the brown-and-white goat Doozie had been so attached to. Of course Bennington had insisted on a ridiculous price because he'd known Gabe needed this goat and not some generic model to calm Doozie. If Gabe had been able to use any old goat, he would have bought one in Jackson, which would have been cheaper and a whole lot less trouble.

The long drive to Colorado and back had given him time to think, though, and to miss Morgan. Missing Morgan was pretty much what he did all the way there and all the way back. He noted with interest that he missed that woman more than riding in competition. A startling discovery.

Whatever radio stations he managed to tune in were playing, as fate would have it, sentimental love songs. Gabe usually liked his music fast and loud, but on this trip sentimental worked for him.

Love songs could get a guy to consider that his attraction to a woman might be about more than sex. He might start realizing that a certain woman, aka Morgan O'Connelli, possessed the honesty and loyalty to go the distance in a relationship. A guy could begin to appreciate a woman's generosity and pluck. A woman who knew how to deal with life's ups and downs.

By the time Gabe was within twenty miles of home, he'd reached a few conclusions. Both the music and the situation with the goat had helped organize his thoughts.

He didn't know how Doozie and the goat had hooked up originally, but they were bonded now. When he'd found the goat, he'd been as miserable-looking as

Doozie. The two of them needed each other. Horn-swaggled wouldn't be content to bunk in with another horse, and Doozie wasn't sharing her stall with any goat off the street.

Whether Gabe liked it or not, he'd formed the same kind of bond with Morgan, although she might not appreciate being compared to a goat. So he'd be the goat and she could be the pretty bay mare. Didn't matter.

What mattered was the bonding concept. Whether they made it official with a preacher or simply hung out together until they were old and gray, he needed this particular woman. She was his chosen mate, and a substitute wasn't going to work for him.

He wasn't so sure about Morgan, though. She was more of a free spirit than he'd realized at first. He'd confused her yearning for a home of her own with a yearning for a husband and kids. She wasn't big on that option.

He knew that for sure, now, because she'd sent him a text message after meeting with his mother. Whenever he stopped for gas or to get something to eat, he looked at it again. He hadn't replied, because a message like that needed to be answered in person.

Saw yr mom. She deserves grandkids. U deserve kids. This is over.

No, it most certainly wasn't. Whether she realized it or not, she was his Doozie, the one he was destined to share a stall with for the rest of their natural lives. He'd figured this out by applying the No-Morgan test. He pictured his life without her in it, which was what she'd suggested in her text message. Totally unacceptable.

Then he pictured his life with Morgan, even if he had to give up the whole marriage-and-kids option, even if he had to scale way back on his riding, and…well, he'd do it. Morgan was more important than any of that.

The trip back from Boulder was eight-plus hours and Gabe got a late start because Bennington dithered around during the loading. So it was after dark when he drove the truck and trailer up next to the barn so he could unload Hornswaggled. He was looking forward to the happiness he would bring both horse and goat, but after he accomplished that reunion, he had one of his own in mind. He planned to unhook the trailer and drive his truck into town.

A single light burned inside the barn, and Gabe noticed that Pam's red Jeep was parked next to the building. He wasn't sure what that was all about. Leading Hornswaggled down the ramp, he headed toward the closed barn doors.

The two dogs, Butch and Sundance, would already be inside and bedded down for the night. Nick made sure of that so they wouldn't be tempted to tangle with the wolves that roamed the hills near the ranch. For the same reason, foals and dams were kept in the barn, and any other vulnerable creature such as Doozie, who was injured.

Holding Hornswaggled's lead rope in his left hand, Gabe approached the barn's double doors and swung open the one on his right. Somebody must have recently oiled the hinges because the door didn't squeak.

That explained why the two people engaged in a

serious lip-lock didn't hear Gabe. He stared at Emmett and Pam executing an R-rated clinch. Emmett had both hands on the seat of Pam's jeans, his fingers spread as he aligned his hips with hers. Fortunately both of them still had all their clothes on, but the way they were glued together, that situation could change any second.

Gabe wasn't sure how to handle this. He needed to put Hornswaggled in Doozie's stall, but in order to do that, he'd have to walk past Emmett and Pam. They might not have noticed him yet, but if he paraded by them leading a goat, they'd notice. Or maybe not, considering the heavy breathing going on.

Hornswaggled took the decision out of his hands by bleating pitifully. Doozie answered with a whinny.

Emmett and Pam leaped apart as if they were both on fire. Which, in a manner of speaking, they were. They'd been consumed by the flames of passion, and now the flames of embarrassment licked at their red faces.

"Uh, sorry." Gabe ducked his head to hide a grin. His matchmaking mother would be tickled to hear about this.

Emmett cleared his throat. "I'd be much obliged if you'd keep this to yourself. It's my fault. I...I overstepped." He glanced at Pam. "Please accept my apologies."

"I will not!" Pam placed her hands on her hips. "You can pretend to be sorry all you want, Emmett Sterling, but you were into it."

Doozie whinnied again and Hornswaggled answered with a loud bleat.

"Gabe needs to get these animals settled." Emmett moved out of the aisle, but kept at least a yard's distance from Pam. "And I...I should be getting to bed."

Pam looked fit to be tied. "By all means, toddle off to bed, Emmett. By yourself." She raised her voice so she could be heard over the now-continuous cries of Doozie and Hornswaggled. "But just remember, it's your own damned stubbornness keeping it that way!" Turning on her heel, she stomped out of the barn. A moment later, her tires spat gravel as she took off.

Emmett blew out a breath and shook his head as he gazed at the wood floor.

Out of respect for all the years Emmett had been like a second father to him, Gabe remained where he was, despite the ruckus. He wanted to give the man a chance to gather the shredded remnants of his pride.

At last the foreman straightened and looked at Gabe. "Time to get this goat and horse together before they wake up the whole damn ranch." He turned and walked toward Doozie's stall.

"Sure thing." Gabe followed, leading a very eager goat.

Goat and horse touched noses, and Hornswaggled wiggled his ears a lot. Doozie let out a huge horsey sigh that told Gabe he'd done the right thing.

Emmett clapped him on the shoulder. "Smart move, son. I'll bet Doozie's gonna be fine now."

"I hope so."

"Guess I'll be heading off to bed."

"Okay." Gabe wasn't heading off to bed, at least not his own.

Emmett paused in the barn doorway. "You'd think someone as old as I am would have more sense."

"I don't think logic and good sense figure into it, Emmett."

"Obviously not. That woman could buy and sell me. I have no business kissing her, and she certainly has no business letting me do it."

Gabe had to process that statement before realizing that Emmett's old-school mentality wouldn't allow him to get involved with a woman who had way more money than he had. "That's kind of a bummer for Pam, don't you think?"

"What do you mean?"

"The way I understand it, she had a two-timing husband who deserved to pay her a bunch of money."

Emmett scowled. "Damn right he did, the bastard. And if she only had that money, it wouldn't be so bad, but there's the inheritance, too. Her parents were loaded."

"Then she needs to donate the entire inheritance to charity."

"What?"

"So you can feel good about dating her." Gabe shrugged. "Seems like the only solution. I'll be happy to suggest it to her if you—"

"You'll do no such thing! She already gives quite a bit to various causes, but the whole inheritance? That's nuts. Some of it needs to go to Nick, anyway, because it's from his grandparents. And Nick will probably have kids, so Pam can't go giving everything away."

Gabe smiled at him. "Exactly. And I see no reason for that poor woman to be penalized because she had the misfortune of being born to rich parents. It's not her fault."

"Penalized?"

"She wants you, Emmett. And from what I just saw, you want her, too. Give the woman a break."

Emmett scrubbed a hand over his face. "I'll think on it, Gabe."

"You do that. And I have to get going. I have something really important to do."

"What's that?"

"Convince Morgan O'Connelli to marry me."

16

IN STARK CONTRAST to the previous evening, tonight Morgan was wearing light blue flannel pj's decorated with teddy bears. She'd bought them on sale because they were designed for a cold winter evening. But in Shoshone, any evening was suitable for flannel, especially if the person wearing it was feeling sorry for herself and needed a hug.

But the hug she needed was the dangerous kind delivered by a certain cowboy who remained on her mind no matter what DVD she watched or how many cups of cocoa she drank. Giving him up was going to be a major pain in the ass. And in the heart. But it was the right thing to do.

He must think so, too, because he hadn't responded to her text message. She'd thought breaking up would be hard to do, just like the old song said, but apparently not. All it took were a few words sent via cell phone and they were done. She should be relieved about that.

Instead she wished there was some way she could know that he was home safe. That kind of thinking had to stop eventually, because she couldn't keep track of his comings and goings in the future. But this one time, when she knew about his road trip, she'd like to get word that he'd successfully brought the goat home and was safe in his own bed.

She'd find out in the next few days. Shoshone was a small town and somebody would mention Gabe's trip while they were eating at the diner, or having drinks at Spirits and Spurs. Or one of the hands from the Last Chance would talk about it when he came into the feed store for supplies. Word would filter to Morgan through the grapevine. But she wanted to know *now*.

As she refilled her mug with cocoa from the pan on the stove, the doorbell rang and she splashed the hot liquid all over. Her hand shook as she put down the mug and grabbed a dishrag to swipe at her pj top.

She knew who was at the door. A visitor at nine-thirty at night could be only one person. Maybe she hadn't broken up with him as completely as she'd thought. But at least he'd come home safe and sound. The tight knot in her stomach loosened.

The doorbell rang a second time. Okay, she'd break up with him in person, and this time she'd make it stick. She wouldn't be the perfect daughter-in-law, and the fallout from that could be huge in a town where the Chances were the reigning royal family. She could kiss her real estate business goodbye.

She opened the door, her speech of farewell on the tip of her tongue.

Gabe obviously had other uses for her tongue, because he swooped in before she could utter a word, crushed her to him and kissed her like a soldier coming home from the war. He held her tight and her struggles were in vain. She'd never quite realized before how strong he was.

Naturally, the longer he spent kissing her, the less she struggled. Kissing Gabe was her second-favorite activity in the world. But she would not allow that activity to lead to her most favorite activity in the world.

At last he came up for air and gazed down at her, his chest heaving. "I missed you so much. You're my Doozie."

"Excuse me? Did that kiss deprive you of oxygen to the brain?"

"Let's go in."

She wasn't quite sure how he accomplished it, but in seconds they were inside her living room and he'd kicked the door shut with his booted foot.

He kept her in a tight grip, refusing to let her go. His expression was endearingly intent. "You're my Doozie. I'm your goat."

She figured out that reuniting the goat and the horse had turned symbolic for him. "Romantic as that sounds, I have to disagree. You haven't found your Doozie yet."

"I have. You're it. Morgan, please marry me. We belong together."

"No, we don't." She pushed futilely at his rock-hard chest. "I meant what I said in my text message. It won't work between us."

"It worked really well the other night." He fitted his pelvis to hers. "I'll bet it could work well tonight, too. And don't think teddy bears will make a difference. I'd want you no matter what you wear."

She could tell that. He was ready to rock and roll,

and naturally, once she was in his arms, so was she. But another romp in her bed would only make things worse for both of them.

Cupping his face in her hands, she looked into those blue, blue eyes. "Listen to me. You're part of a legacy. What you need is a ranch wife who doesn't mind sending you off to compete while she raises the grandchildren your mother so desperately wants."

"Nick can be in charge of producing kids."

She shook her head. "Not just Nick. All of you. You're destined to carry on the Chance name, and I understand that. But when it comes to women suited to marry the Chance boys, I don't fit the mold. I don't want to be a disappointment to your mother, but mostly, I don't want to be a disappointment to you."

"You couldn't be."

"Oh, yes, I could." Her heart ached, but this had to be said. "Not at first, when the sex is great and I can travel a little bit with you. But we can only be newlyweds for so long before everyone starts asking 'what's next?' The obvious answer is children."

His jaw tightened. "If you don't want them, then we won't have any."

"Be honest with yourself. You were envious of Nick and Dominique when they were planning their house. How will you feel when they have a baby? And your mom gets all weepy and happy about it?"

Uncertainty danced in his eyes. "You could change your mind."

She wanted to keep that feeling of uncertainty alive, for his sake. "Maybe I'll change my mind, but this is a big issue, Gabe. We can't base a life on the possibility that I'll get excited about having kids. I might not. Look, neither of us went into this with plans for a future together. Don't force it. Let me go."

The pain in his expression nearly toppled her resolve. "I don't want to."

"And I don't want to keep this up. I...I'm starting to care for you." She didn't have the courage to use the *L*-word at this point in time. "If we're headed down a dead-end street, then we need to turn back now, before we crash."

He swallowed. "Morgan..."

"You know I'm right. Just go. Go now, before we hurt each other any more. I'm not the person you need."

"And you don't want to be."

This was the hard part. "No, I don't." She longed to close her eyes and block out his tortured gaze, but that wouldn't be fair. Flinching would indicate she wasn't sure. And she was. She *was*.

"All right, then." Releasing her, he turned toward the door. "But I still think you're my Doozie."

"You got the goat okay?"

"Yeah. Doozie was overjoyed to see him." Gabe opened the door and walked out, dejection and defeat in every line of his body.

She pressed her lips together to keep from calling him back. But she loved him too much to hand out false hope. Someday he'd find a woman better suited to him, and then he'd thank Morgan for sending him away tonight.

If only she could take more comfort in that.

GABE DIDN'T REMEMBER much about the drive home. He sat in the circular driveway for a while, trying to summon the energy to go inside, but everything seemed so pointless now. Unfortunately he understood exactly what Morgan was talking about, and she was right.

He could see himself marrying her with the promise that he didn't care about kids, just so he could satisfy this driving need to be with her. But he did care about kids, and he'd marry her with the secret wish that she'd change. If she didn't…they'd be in trouble.

Slamming his hands against the truck's steering wheel, he cursed Morgan's parents for souring her on the concept of having children. Not much could be done about that now, though. He might as well get on with his life.

When he went inside, he noticed that someone had left a lamp burning in the living room. Probably his mother, so he wouldn't stumble around in the dark. He walked over to turn it off before going upstairs.

Jack's voice startled him. "Did you drive into town to see Morgan?"

He looked over and found his big brother in one of the leather easy chairs that circled a round coffee table in front of the fireplace. A bottle of whiskey sat on an end table beside him and he held a shot glass in his hand. Gabe wasn't in the mood to listen to another of Jack's tirades on the subject of Morgan. He started to leave the room.

"I was wrong about her," Jack said.

Gabe paused and waited for trumpets to herald this miracle—Jack admitting he'd made an error in judgment.

"Don't look so shocked." Jack drained his shot glass

and set it on the table next to the bottle. "I've been wrong once or twice in my life."

"I'm aware of that. I just never expected you to say so."

"Yeah, well…get ready, because here comes another one. I was wrong about paying for your competition, too. I was forgetting something major. It makes Sarah happy to know you're out there using the skills Dad taught you. That's worth whatever it costs, and if you help sell a few horses in the process, so much the better."

"Okay." At the moment, Gabe didn't give a shit about riding in competitions, but he wasn't going to say that.

"You might actually get Top Drawer into the Hall of Fame, which would be a bonus. Besides, you're a tax write-off."

"Woo-hoo." Gabe made a circle in the air with his finger.

"Do you understand me? I'm saying you're clear to get back out there."

"Great." He couldn't believe how little that meant compared to losing Morgan. He should be grateful, though, because competing would provide a way to take his mind off her.

"You don't sound very happy about it. Is something wrong? I mean, you're home kinda early. Is Morgan sick or something?"

"No. It's…it's over. We're done."

Jack let loose with a string of colorful swear words. "It's my fault, isn't it? For being such an a-hole."

"No, it's not your fault. Everything doesn't have to be about you, Jack."

He shrugged. "If you say so. Then what's the problem?"

"I really don't want to talk about—"

"Aw, hell, Gabe. Who else you got to bounce things off of? Nick's sailing around on cloud nine, so you don't want to lay this on him. That leaves me and Sarah, and it's dangerous to give your mother too much information."

Gabe couldn't help laughing at the truth of that. And in that instant, he was transported back to a happier time when Jack had been the go-to guy for problems with women. Both Gabe and Nick had depended on Jack's worldly knowledge to get them through the maze of male-female relationships.

Except Jack hadn't done so well in that department himself. He'd walked away from a wonderful woman and Gabe figured Josie was still hurting over it. She wasn't dating anyone else, either.

Jack waved a hand toward the chair next to him. "You're not gonna sleep, so you might as well sit here instead of pacing around in your room."

With a sigh of resignation, Gabe sank down on the smooth leather of the chair next to Jack's.

"Want a drink?"

Gabe shook his head.

"So why'd she dump you?"

"Who says she dumped me?"

"It's not rocket science, little brother. You look like you've been tromped on by a bull."

"After raising her brothers and sisters, she's sick of

the whole kid thing. She may never want any of her own."

"And you do?"

Gabe scrubbed a hand over his face. "Yeah. Someday. I tried to convince myself it didn't matter, but she was smarter than that. She knew it would matter sooner or later."

"Points for the lady."

"I know. It's just that…I think she's the one for me."

"So you're in love with her."

Gabe had been avoiding admitting that to himself, because it would make everything worse. "Yeah. Good thing I didn't tell her that."

"*Good thing?* Are you insane? You asked her to marry you and didn't say you loved her first?"

"I thought she'd figure that out."

"Dear God." Jack shook his head. "You're even dumber than I thought."

"Don't go calling me dumb. At least I proposed. You're the wiseass who walked away from the best thing that ever happened to you."

Jack stared at him in silence before taking a deep breath. "Could be. But that can't be fixed anytime soon. You, on the other hand, need to strike while the iron is hot."

"Forget it. She sent me packing."

"Doesn't matter. You have two problems to overcome." Jack held up his forefinger. "One, you made a serious tactical error in not declaring your love. We can fix that." He held up his middle finger. "Two, she doesn't want kids. But from what Sarah told me about her, she—"

"You talked to Mom about her?"

"Sarah talked to me. Called me on the carpet, actually. We got a few things straightened out. But your lady's family moved all over God's creation while the kids were young, right?"

"Uh-huh, which is why she's so determined to stay in Shoshone forever."

"There you go. When she was dealing with her sisters and brothers, I'm betting the family was isolated. No grandparents, aunties or uncles around to help out."

Gabe thought about that. "Sounds right."

"But at the Last Chance, there's Sarah, Mary Lou, Emmett, the other cowhands, Pam, Nick and Dominique, even Jack the hard-ass. Around here, a kid's feet will never touch the ground!"

"You're right." For the first time since leaving Morgan's house, Gabe saw a glimmer of hope. "You think she'll buy that?"

"One way to find out." Jack stood. "Let's go."

"Go where?"

"To Morgan's house. You drive. I've had a few."

MORGAN SAT UP in bed, pounded the pillow into shape and flopped down again. She had two appointments in the morning and another one in the afternoon. If she didn't get to sleep soon, she'd have a tough time being perky.

That would be bad. She counted on perky. It was one

of her selling tools. But this whole miserable situation with Gabe had sucked out all her perky.

Not her adrenaline, though. When the doorbell rang, she leaped out of bed as if she'd been shot from a cannon and stood in the middle of her dark bedroom gulping for air.

It had to be Gabe, but she simply couldn't face him again. Opening that door would send her right back into his arms, and she wasn't going there. She was tough, but not that tough.

Of course Gabe wasn't the kind to give up, so the doorbell kept ringing…and ringing…

Finally she couldn't take it anymore. She walked into the living room but didn't turn on any lights. Consequently she stubbed her toe on the leg of the sofa as she made her way to a double-hung window at the front of the house. She swore under her breath as she hobbled to the window, which she'd left partway open with the security latch on.

Crouching down, she pulled aside the curtains and called out through the opening at the bottom of the window. "Go away!"

"Morgan, it's Jack."

Jack? She raced to unlock the door. "Is Gabe okay?" Then she saw both of them standing on her small porch. She'd have to be dead not to appreciate the sight they presented in their boots, bun-hugging jeans, fitted shirts and Stetsons cocked at a jaunty angle.

Still, she had her priorities. "You scared me half to death. Now go away." She started to close the door.

"I think you have termites," Jack said.

"What?"

"Termites." He elbowed Gabe in the ribs.

Morgan sighed. "I get it. You're making stuff up to keep me from closing the door. Goodnight, boys."

"No, seriously! Feels spongy." Jack jumped up and down and the boards squeaked. "Hear that?" He elbowed Gabe a second time.

"Look, I don't know what you're up to, but—"

"For God's sake, Gabe!" Jack shoved him forward. "Say it!"

Gabe swallowed. "Morgan, I love you."

That cowboy sure knew how to deliver a sucker punch. She got chills followed by a warm, sweet feeling spreading through her like rivers of hot fudge. She still couldn't marry him, but she'd never forget this moment.

She took a shaky breath. "That's…that's nice to hear."

Jack clapped his brother on the shoulder. "But that's not all, is it, Gabe?"

"No, it's not." Gabe focused those blue eyes directly on her. "I should have told you that first, before I brought up the whole marriage-and-babies subject, before I said you were my Doozie. I—"

"Hold it." Jack hooked an arm around Gabe's shoulders and drew him aside. "This enterprise is running off the rails. *Doozie?* What in hell does your lame horse have to do with anything?"

"We belong together, just like Doozie and Hornswaggled, except I didn't think Morgan would want to be compared to a goat, plus she's a woman, and Doozie's a mare, so—"

"Good night, Irene." Jack glanced over at Morgan. "Could you excuse us for a sec?"

"Sure." Morgan watched as the two brothers put their heads together, their voices hushed but intense. Meanwhile her resolve was melting faster than an ice cube in a microwave. How was she supposed to resist a campaign like this, where Gabe's earnest but slightly goofy appeal was being coached by his older brother? She'd never seen anything so endearing in her life.

But if she caved, could she be the wife Gabe needed? That was the sticking point. Yet how she loved the man. She loved him even more for stumbling through this when he probably expected total rejection. He'd made himself so vulnerable.

He and Jack must have settled on a strategy, because they came out of their huddle and walked toward her again. Gabe took off his hat and mopped his forehead with his sleeve. If she'd ever doubted that he was fully engaged in this struggle, she doubted it no longer.

He put on his hat and stood before her, his legs spread a little as if he were bracing for what might come. "About the kid thing."

"It's still an issue, Gabe." She owed him the truth.

"I know, but—"

"Uncle Jack, standing by." Jack balanced on his toes and waved at her.

Gabe turned to him. "I'm handling it, Jack."

"Just making sure you stay on track, bro."

"I know what to say, so butt out." Gabe faced her again. "I'm not putting pressure on you, Morgan."

She nodded. "Good." Because the least little pressure would send her into his arms.

"But I want you to consider something. When you were responsible for all those kids, you had no other relatives to lighten the load."

"No. We were always on the move."

"Exactly. But as Jack pointed out to me, our kid would have tons of people—my mom, Mary Lou, Nick and Dominique, Emmett, Pam and Jack, believe it or not. Even the cowhands would want to take a turn. You'd have babysitters coming out your ears."

"The kid's feet will never touch the ground!" Jack chortled.

"Our kid." Morgan said it softly, almost afraid to imagine it, but…suddenly the idea wasn't some abstract concept that she could easily reject. He was discussing a baby who would have his hair and eyes, or her hair and eyes, or his hair and her eyes. Their kid.

"You probably need some time to think about it." His gaze was tender, filled with the love he'd so recently declared.

"Don't give her time to think, idiot!" Jack waved both arms in the air. "Can't you see she's waffling? Close the deal!"

Morgan stepped forward. "I'll close the deal. I love you, Gabriel Archibald Chance. Let's get married and have a baby who will torture Uncle Jack."

Gabe's smile lit up the darkness. "Yeah, let's." He pulled her into his arms. "I vote we celebrate that decision."

"Hey!" Jack called out. "Don't forget about me! I need to go home, y'know. And I shouldn't be driving."

"Then go knock on Josie's door," Gabe said.

Morgan had no idea how Jack responded to that suggestion, because Gabe had maneuvered her into the house by then and had started on the buttons of her teddy-bear flannels.

"Did I tell you how much I love teddy bears?" he murmured in her ear.

"No." She tugged him into her bedroom.

"Not nearly as much as I love you." And with that, they tumbled onto the mattress.

After a lifetime of wandering, Morgan finally knew where she belonged—here in Gabe's arms. Someday, when the time was right, their lovemaking would create a Last Chance baby. And the kid's feet would never touch the ground.

* * * * *

COMING NEXT MONTH

Available July 27, 2010

#555 TWICE THE TEMPTATION
Cara Summers
Forbidden Fantasies/Encounters

#556 CLAIMED!
Vicki Lewis Thompson
Sons of Chance

#557 THE RENEGADE
Rhonda Nelson
Men Out of Uniform

#558 THE HEAT IS ON
Jill Shalvis
American Heroes

#559 CATCHING HEAT
Lisa Renee Jones

#560 DOUBLE PLAY
Joanne Rock
The Wrong Bed

REQUEST YOUR FREE BOOKS!

HARLEQUIN®

2 FREE NOVELS PLUS 2 FREE GIFTS!

Blaze™

Red-hot reads!

HARLEQUIN®

A *Romance*

FOR EVERY MOOD™

Spotlight on

— Heart & Home —

Heartwarming romances
where love can happen
right when you least expect it.

See the next page to enjoy a sneak peek
from Harlequin® American Romance®,
a Heart and Home series.

*Five hunky Texas single fathers—five stories from
Cathy Gillen Thacker's* LONE STAR DADS *miniseries.
Here's an excerpt from the latest, THE MOMMY PROPOSAL
from Harlequin American Romance.*

"I hear you work miracles," Nate Hutchinson drawled.
Brooke Mitchell had just stepped into his lavishly appointed
office in downtown Fort Worth, Texas.

"Sometimes, I do." Brooke smiled and took the sexy
financier's hand in hers, shook it briefly.

"Good." Nate looked her straight in the eye. "Because
I'm in need of a home makeover—fast. The son of an old
friend is coming to live with me."

She was still tingling from the feel of his warm palm.
"Temporarily or permanently?"

"If all goes according to plan, I'll adopt Landry by
summer's end."

Brooke had heard the founder of Nate Hutchinson
Financial Services was eligible, wealthy and generous to a
fault. She hadn't known he was in the market for a family,
but she supposed she shouldn't be surprised. But Brooke
had figured a man as successful and handsome as Nate
would want one the old-fashioned way. *Not that this was
any of her business...*

"So what's the child like?" she asked crisply, trying not
to think how the marine-blue of Nate's dress shirt deepened
the hue of his eyes.

"I don't know." Nate took a seat behind his massive
antique mahogany desk. He relaxed against the smooth
leather of the chair. "I've never met him."

"Yet you've invited this kid to live with you permanently?"

"It's complicated. But I'm sure it's going to be fine."

Obviously Nate Hutchinson knew as little about teenage

boys as he did about decorating. But that wasn't her problem.
Finding a way to do the assignment without getting the least
bit emotionally involved was.

*Find out how a young boy brings Nate and Brooke
together in THE MOMMY PROPOSAL,
coming August 2010 from Harlequin American Romance.*